George Hembert Westley

For Love's Sweet Sake

Selected Poems of Love in All Moods

George Hembert Westley

For Love's Sweet Sake
Selected Poems of Love in All Moods

ISBN/EAN: 9783337407803

Printed in Europe, USA, Canada, Australia, Japan

Cover: Foto ©Andreas Hilbeck / pixelio.de

More available books at **www.hansebooks.com**

FOR LOVE'S SWEET SAKE

Selected Poems of Love in all Moods

EDITED BY

G. HEMBERT WESTLEY

"THE STORY OF ALL STORIES, SWEET AND OLD,
SWEETEST TO LOVERS THE LAST TIME 'TIS TOLD."

BOSTON
LEE AND SHEPARD PUBLISHERS
1899

To

MY DEAR FRIEND AIMÉE

Oft have I gathered flowers for thee
   In the fair, sweet summer time,
And pretty shells by the shimmering sea
   When our youth was in its prime.

So in memory of that yesteryear
   Which did all so happy prove,
I have gathered this fragrant posy, dear,
   From the flowery fields of Love.

                            G. H. W.

ACKNOWLEDGMENTS

FOR kind permission to use a number of the poems in this collection the editor offers his sincere thanks to the publishing houses that have extended this courtesy to his publishers and himself. Credit is hereby given to Houghton, Mifflin, and Company, by special arrangement with whom poems by Longfellow, T. B. Aldrich, and J. G. Saxe are used; to G. P. Putnam's Sons for the poem, "The Rosary," by Robert Cameron Rogers; to the Frederick A. Stokes Company for three poems by Mary Berri Chapman; to Little, Brown, and Company for the poem, "Two Truths," by Helen Hunt Jackson, the poem, "Fate," by Susan Marr Spalding; and to De Wolfe, Fiske, and Company for two poems by Owen Innsley; also to Miss Helen M. Reeve Aldrich, sister of the late very promising young poetess, Anne Reeve Aldrich; and to Barton Gray, the Southern poet. The editor has tried to be very careful in this matter of permission, and if, through being unable to trace a fugitive poem to its original source, he has failed to give due credit to any poet or publishing house, he herewith and beforehand presents his most humble apologies.

G. H. W.

BOSTON, April, 1899.

CONTENTS

ix

INDEX

I

LOVE'S MORNING

Oh there's nothing half so sweet in life
As love's young dream.

THOMAS MOORE.

None without hope e'er loved the brightest fair ;
But Love can hope where Reason would despair.

LORD LYTTELTON.

Oh Love ! young Love ! bound in thy rosy band,
Let sage or cynic prattle as he will,
These hours, and these alone, redeem Life's years of ill.

LORD BYRON.

FOR LOVE'S SWEET SAKE

"I LOVE YOU, DEAR"

"I LOVE you, dear."
　　There is no phrase so worn and old
In all the world, nor one so sweet
To lover's lips or maiden's ear
As this refrain, "I love you, dear."

　　　　"I love you, dear."
There is no change as time goes on;
No new words seem to mean so much
As when they're uttered fondly near,
In trembling tones, "I love you, dear."

　　　　"I love you, dear."
No night so dark, no day so long
But hope brings comfort to the heart,
If only "some one" standeth near
To murmur low, "I love you, dear."

MY LOVE

MY love's worth all the world to me:
  Her walk to others' dance is light.
When she comes by, the sun rides high,
  And when she's past, 'tis night!

Her gentle voice, that bids "Good day,"
  Is music that my soul loves best;
Her deep set eyes, her low replies,
  The dreams that haunt my rest.

Her presence, like fresh morning showers
  Gives to all things refreshing grace;
If she but stoop, sweet buds that droop,
  Gaze up into her face.

That May-day face — where nothing lives
  That is not bright, for long together;
Thoughts come and go, like winds that blow
  The clouds in golden weather.

Life's passing shades have scarcely chill'd
  The gladness of her spirit's light —
O when she's by, the sun seems high,
  And when she's past, 'tis night!

HAMILTON AÏDÉ

SHE IS SO PRETTY

SHE is so pretty, the girl I love,
  Her eyes are tender and deep and blue
As the summer night in the skies above,

4

As violets seen through a mist of dew.
How can I hope then her heart to gain ?
She is so pretty, and I am so plain !

She is so pretty, so fair to see !
   Scarcely she's counted her nineteenth spring,
Fresh, and blooming, and young — ah me !
   Why do I thus her praises sing ?
Surely from me 'tis a senseless strain,
She is so pretty, and I am so plain !

She is pretty, so sweet and dear
   There's many a lover who loves her well;
I may not hope, I can only fear,
   Yet shall I venture my love to tell ? . . .
Ah! I have pleaded, and not in vain —
Though she's so pretty, and I'm so plain.
                   From Beranger, by ETHEL GREY

KISSING INDUCEMENTS

THE clouds that rest on the mountain's breast
   Are kissed by the viewless air ;
And the western breeze doth kiss the trees
   And woo the flowerets fair.
And the weeping willows are kissed by the billows.
   And the day-star kisses the sea —
Then why not, dearest, loveliest, fairest,
   Give a kiss to me ?

The bright moonbeam doth kiss the stream
    The hill and the peaceful vale,
And the shady bower, at even's hour,
    Is woo'd by the nightingale.
And the lily and rose, and each flower that blows
    Are kissed by the roving bee,
Then why not, dearest, loveliest, fairest,
    Give a kiss to me ?

WISHES

I WISH, my sweet, thou wert a rose,
    And I a golden bee, to sip
The honey dew that doth repose
    In balmy kisses on thy lip.

I wish thine eyes were violets blue,
    And I a wandering western breeze,
To press thee with my wings of dew
    And melt them into ecstasies !

I wish thou wert a golden curl,
    And I the myrtle-wreath that bound it ;
I wish thou wert a peerless pearl,
    And I the casket to surround it !

I wish thou wert a lucid star,
    And I the atmosphere about thee —
But if we must be as we are
    Dearest, I cannot live without thee.

HENRY HALLORAN

6

I LOVE THEE

I LOVE thee; why, I cannot tell,
  A thousand nameless winning ways
Around thee weave their magic spell
  And make words poor to speak thy praise.

I love thee; not because thine eyes
  Are matched by heaven's celestial blue,
But in thy trustful look there lies
  The unspoken promise to be true.

I love thee for some subtle charm
  That seems to draw my heart to thine;
Thy voice and look my fears disarm,
  And tell me thou art only mine.

I love thee; not for wealth or fame —
  No worldly wish holds thought of thee;
And since thy heart reveals the same,
  How bright with hope our lives may be!

M. A. BAINES

MY QUEEN

SHE must be courteous, she must be holy,
  Pure in spirit, that maiden I love;
Whether her birth be noble or lowly,
  I care no more than the spirits above.
And I'll give my heart to my lady's keeping,
  And ever her strength on mine shall lean,
And the stars shall fall and the angels be weeping
  Ere I cease to love her, my Queen, my Queen!

From an Old Song

7

DANCE SONG

HOW could I, sweet, have sung another song?
　　To you there was but one for me to sing;
But one, and ah! you know it all so long
That now I fear it seems an idle·thing —
　　With tireless feet, with tireless feet
　　Dance on, dance on! I love you, sweet.

How shall I whisper, dear, another word?
Do I not hold you, breathing breast to breast?
My heart has naught to say yours has not heard,
Of all Love's speeches, silence is the best —
　　I will not fear, I will not fear.
　　Dance on, dance on! I love you, dear.

F. W. L. ADAMS

SWEETHEART

THERE is a little bird that sings:
　　"Sweetheart! sweetheart! sweetheart!"
I know not what his name may be,
I only know he pleases me,
As loud he sings — and thus sings he —
　　"Sweetheart! sweetheart! sweetheart!"

I've heard him sing on soft spring days
　　"Sweetheart! sweetheart! sweetheart!"
And when the sky was dark above,
And wintry winds had stripped the grove,
He still poured forth his words of love —
　　"Sweetheart! sweetheart! sweetheart!"

3

And like that bird my heart, too, sings
  " Sweetheart! sweetheart! sweetheart!"
When heav'n is dark or bright and blue,
When trees are bare or leaves are new,
It thus sings on — and sings of you —
  " Sweetheart! sweetheart! sweetheart!"

What need of other words than these:
  " Sweetheart! sweetheart! sweetheart!"
If I should sing the whole year long,
My love would not be shown more strong,
Than by this short and simple song —
  " Sweetheart! sweetheart! sweetheart!"
                                    AUGUSTUS GREVILLE

SINGING OF YOU

I'M singing of you when the darkness is falling,
  Falling from heaven and blotting its blue;
Singing of you when the night winds are calling,
  Thralling my heart, that is singing of you.

I'm singing of you when the robins are waking,
  Slaking their thirst in the glistening dew;
Singing of you when the May dawn is breaking,
  Taking my thought to you, singing of you.

I'm singing of you with a song of love, ringing,
  Winging its way to you; telling you true;
Singing of you and the bliss you are bringing,
  Flinging my life to you, singing of you.

SINCE WE PARTED

SINCE we parted yester eve,
  I do love thee, love, believe,
Twelve times dearer, twelve hours longer,
One dream deeper, one night stronger,
One sun surer, — thus much more
Than I loved thee, love, before.

OWEN MEREDITH

LOVE SONG

TO look for thee — sigh for thee — cry for thee,
    Under my breath ;
To clasp but a shade where thy head hath laid.
    It is death.

To long for thee — yearn for thee — burn for thee —
    Sorrow and strife ! —
But to have thee — and hold thee — and fold thee —
    It is life — it is life !

LOVE AND PITY

LOVE came a beggar to her gate,
  The night was drear, the hour was late,
And through the gloom she heard his moan
Where at the gate he stood alone.

His rounded form in rags was clad,
His weeping eyes were wan and sad;
But hid beneath his garb of woe
He bore his arrows and his bow.

She wept to see the beggar weep,
She bade him in her bosom sleep,
His wretched plight allayed her fears,
She kissed and bathed him with her tears.

The merry eyes began to glow,
The rosy hand essayed the bow,
The rough disguise was cast aside,
And laughing Love for mercy cried.

Love came a beggar to her gate,
More wisely than with pomp and state;
For who hath woman's pity won
May count love's siege and battle done.

WERE I THY BRIDE

WERE I thy bride,
   Then all the world beside
Were not too wide
   To hold my wealth of love —
      Were I thy bride !
Upon thy breast
My loving head would rest
As in her nest
   The tender turtle-dove —
      Were I thy bride !

This heart of mine
Would be one heart with thine,
And in that shrine
   Our happiness would dwell —
      Were I thy bride !

And all day long
Our lives should be a song;
No grief, no wrong
    Should make my heart rebel
        Were I thy bride !

The rose's sigh
Were as a carrion's cry
To lullaby
    Such as I'd sing to thee
        Were I thy bride !
A feather's press
Were leaden heaviness
To my caress —
    Ah, love, how sweet 'twould be
        Were I thy bride !

Old Song

AT THE DANCE

MY queen is tired and craves surcease
    Of twanging string and clamorous brass;
I lean against the mantelpiece,
    And watch her in the glass.

One whom I see not where I stand
    Fans her and talks in whispers low;
Her loose locks flutter as his hand
    Moves lightly to and fro.

He begs a flower; her finger-tips
    Stray round a rose half veiled in lace;
She grants the boon with smiling lips,
    Her clear eyes read his face.

12

I cannot look, my sight grows dim —
  While Fate allots unequally,
The living woman's self to him,
  The mirrored form to me.

AUGUSTA DE GRUCHY

ROSE SONG

SUNNY breath of roses,
  Roses white and red,
Rosy bud and rose leaf
  From the blossom shed !
Goes my darling flying
  All the garden through,
Laughing she eludes me,
  Laughing I pursue.

Now to pluck the rosebud,
  Now to pluck the rose,
(Hand a sweeter blossom)
  Stopping as she goes :
What but this contents her,
  Laughing in her flight,
Pelting with red roses,
  Pelting with the white.

Roses round me flying,
  Roses in my hair,
I to snatch them trying,
  Darling, have a care !

Lips are so like flowers
I might snatch at those,
Redder than the rose leaves,
Sweeter than the rose.

WILLIAM SAWYER

A VALENTINE

IF I were a leaf on a tree,
  And you were the wind from the west;
Would you waft me away in your strong embrace,
  And pillow my head on your breast ?

If you were the sun in his strength,
  And I were a morsel of dew;
Would you lift me away from my low estate,
  And carry me nearer you ?

If you were the King among men,
  And only my love were mine,
Would you single me out from all maidens on earth,
  To choose me your Valentine ?

MARY T. REILEY

A LOVE TEST

SWEET, do you ask me if you love or no?
  Soon will your answers to my questions show:
If in your cheeks hot blushes come and go
Like rose leaves shaken on new-fallen snow;
If tender sorrows in your heart arise
And sudden teardrops tremble in your eyes;
If from my presence you would sigh to part,
Believe me, darling, I have touched your heart.

LOVE'S ROSES

If when I speak your blue-veined eyelids sink
And veil the thoughts you scarcely dare to think :
If when I greet you, hardly you reply,
And when we part, but breathe a faint "Good-by ! "
If your sweet face to mine you cannot raise,
Yet fear not so to meet another's gaze ;
If all these things to make you glad combine,
Believe me, darling, that your heart is mine.

From the German of Carl Herloszsohn

LOVE'S PUNISHMENTS

OH, if my love offended me
      And we had words together,
To show her I would master be,
    I'd whip her with a feather !

If then she, like a naughty girl,
    Would tyranny declare it,
I'd give my love a cross of pearl
    And make her always bear it !

If still she tried to sulk and sigh
    And throw away my posies,
I'd catch my darling on the sly
    And smother her with roses !

And if she dared her lips to pout,
    Like many pert young misses,
I'd wind my arm her waist about
    And punish her — with kisses.

J. ASHBY-STERRY

15

THE END OF THE ROMANCE

OUR love was like most other loves;
　　A little glow, a little shiver,
A rosebud, and a pair of gloves,
　　And "Fly not yet" — upon the river;
Some jealousy of some one's heir,
　　Some talk of dying broken-hearted,
A miniature, a lock of hair,
　　The usual vows, — and then we parted.

We parted; months and years rolled by;
　　We met again four summers after;
Our parting was all sob and sigh;
　　Our meeting was all mirth and laughter:
For in my heart's most secret cell
　　There had been many other lodgers;
And she was not the ballroom's belle,
　　But only — Mrs. Something Rogers.
　　　　　　　　　　　WINTHROP M. PRAED

THE WELCOME

COME in the evening, or come in the morning, —
　　Come when you're looked for, or come without
　　warning, —
Kisses and welcome you'll find here before you,
And the oftener you come here the more I'll adore you!
　　　　　　　　　　THOMAS OSBORNE DAVIS

LOVE'S ROSES

SIR RQNALD'S sword was brave and keen,
  In the sunlight flashing bright;
But Oh ! so deathly grim, I ween,
  I could not bear the sight.

Sir Ronald's heart was true and leal,
  So manly, high, and bold;
But ah ! full like his gleaming steel
  All stern it seemed and cold.

And so I took the roses fair,
  And wreathed the ghastly blade;
All peacefully they nestled there,
  No more was I afraid.

And lo ! the knight by some sweet art,
  Grew warm toward me and kind —
I little knew that 'round his heart
  The flowers of love I twined.

W. F. Gregory

LONG YEARS AGO

ALL for a pretty girlish face,
  Two cheeks of rosy hue,
Two laughing eyes of vermeil tint
  And eyes of heaven's blue.

All for a little dimpled chin,
  A round throat snowy fair,
A darling mouth to dream upon
  And glorious golden hair.

All for a tender cooing voice,
  And gentle fluttering sighs;
All for the promise made to me
  By story-telling eyes.

All for that pretty girlish face,
  For a hand as white as snow,
I dreamed a foolish dream of love
  Long, long years ago.

A BIRTHDAY GREETING

WHAT shall I give you, sweet, to-day —
  A wreath to deck your sunny hair —
A wreath of roses, fresh and fair,
  Breathing the pure and scented air
Of balmy May ?
No — I'll not give you that to-day,
For roses, dear, will fade away !

What shall I give you, sweet, to-day —
   A costly robe of silk brocade,
   By lovely fingers deftly made
   That you might fitly be arrayed
To wield your sway ?
No — I'll not give you that to-day.
For silk, dear heart, will wear away !

What shall I give you, sweet, to-day —
   A jewelled chaplet, or a ring
   Worthy the ransom of a king,
   A coronet — some trifling thing
For hours of play ?
No — I'll not give you gems to-day,
For gems are ofttimes stol'n away !

What shall I give you, sweet, to-day,
   That shall with you through strife and stress,
   Through bitter failure, sweet success,
   Through mirth, through dread unhappiness
Forever stay ?
Sweet, at your feet I lay to-day
My love — for that will last alway !

HENRY EDLIN

LOVE'S GIFTS

I GAVE my love a fan before she knew
   I loved her more than dared my tongue impart :
She took it with a smile ; but saw not through
   Mine eyes that I had given her first my heart.
O fan, how envied I the happy air
Thou brought'st a-wooing to that face so fair !

I gave her flowers — Nature's living gems;
   The likest thing on earth to her I've known!
All beauty, grace, and sweetness; diadems
   To bind her brows, and posies for her zone.
O happy flowers, what had I given to lie,
Like ye, on that fair breast, though but to die!

I gave my love a ring — no costly prize;
   Naught but a little simple hoop of gold.
She placed it on her finger with sweet sighs,
   And sweeter looks, that made my tongue more
      bold.
"O happy ring upon that hand to shine!
O lovely lady, would that hand were mine!"

My love gave me — a kiss. O wanton air,
   I envy thee no more! O luckless flowers,
I breathe fresh life upon that bosom fair,
   Where ye but perish in a few short hours.
O ring, a finger thou dost clasp alone!
My arms encircle all — for she is all mine own!

ON RECEIVING A WHITE PINK

DEAR little fair and fragrant flower,
    A double sweetness lingers
Around thy smooth and slender stem
    Because my darling's fingers
Have culled thee from the parent stem,
    Because his lips have pressed thee,
And well I know ere thou wert sent
    With words of love he blessed thee.

Sweet blossom, on thy snowy leaves,
    And with thy fragrance blending,
A message comes of tender love,
    All other love transcending;
And as I kiss each tiny bud,
    (For every leaf I treasure)
I wonder if my darling knows
    He gave me such a pleasure.

                            " VIOLA "

THE ENCHANTMENT

I DID but look and love awhile,
    'Twas but for one half-hour;
Then to resist I had no will,
    And now I have no power.

To sigh and wish is all my ease, —
    Sighs which do heat impart,
Enough to melt the coldest ice,
    Yet cannot warm your heart. .

O would your pity give my heart
  One corner of your breast,
'Twould learn of yours the winning art
  And quickly steal the rest.

THOMAS OTWAY

TO —

WARM summer dwells upon thy cheeks
    And in thy dancing eyes.
But, fair one, in thy little heart
  Cold, frosty winter lies.

Yet these, I think, as years grow on
  Will play a different part;
Then winter on thy cheeks shall be
  And summer in thy heart.

HEINRICH HEINE

THE DOUBT RESOLVED

TO go or stay, I scarcely knew,
    Perplexed by mandates twain.
For while my love pronounced "Adieu"
  Her aspect said "Remain."
'Twixt what I saw and what I heard
  My judgment wavered quite, —
Whether she meant by glance or word
  To part us or unite.

22

But now each lover I advise,
  Like me to make his choice;
In duty to his lady's eyes,
  To disregard her voice.
Such orbs with kinder light are filled
  The nearer we adore,
And pouting lips, if bravely stilled,
  Will banish us no more.

A HEART FOR EVERY ONE

OH, there's a heart for every one,
  If every one could find it;
Then up and seek ere youth is gone,
  Whate'er the toil, ne'er mind it;
For if you chance to meet at last
  With that one heart intended
To be a blessing unsurpassed,
  Till life itself is ended,
How would you prize the labor done,
  How grieve if you resigned it;
For there's a heart for every one
  If every one could find it!

CHARLES SWAIN

THE FIRST KISS

O HAPPY hush of heart to heart!
O moment molten through with bliss!
O Love, delaying long to part
That first, fast, individual kiss!
Whereon two lives on glowing lips
Hang claspt, each feeling fold in fold,
Like daisies closed with crimson tips,
That sleep about a heart of gold.

OWEN MEREDITH

HALF-HEARTED

IF I could love thee, Love, a little more,
If thy fair love outlived the brief sweet rose—
If in my golden field were all thy store,
And all my joy within thy garden close,—
Then would I pray my heart to be full fond
Forever and a little bit beyond.

If daffodil and primrose were not frail,
If snowdrop died not ere the dying day—
If I were true as Daphnis in the tale,
And thou could'st love as Juliet in the play,—
Then would I teach my heart to be full fond
Forever and a little bit beyond.

But since I fear I am but wayward true,
And wayward false, fair love, thou seem'st to be—
Since I some day must sigh for something new
And each day thou for life's monotony,—
Prithee, stay here ere yet we grow too fond,
And let me pass a little bit beyond.

From Macmillan

COMEDY

THEY parted, with clasps of hand,
  And kisses, and burning tears.
They met in a foreign land,
  After some twenty years:

Met as acquaintances meet,
  Smilingly, tranquil-eyed —
Not even the least little beat
  Of the heart upon either side!

They chatted of this and that,
  The nothings that make up life;
She in a Gainsborough hat,
  And he in black for his wife.

Ah, what a comedy this!
  Neither was hurt, it appears:
Yet once she had leaned to his kiss,
  And once he had known her tears!
                    THOMAS BAILEY ALDRICH

HALF–WAY IN LOVE

YOU have come then; how very clever!
  I thought you would scarcely try;
I was doubtful myself — however,
  You have come, and so have I.

How cool it is here, and pretty!
  You are vexed; I'm afraid I'm late;
You've been waiting — Oh, what a pity!
  And its almost half-past eight.

So it is; I can hear it striking
    Out there in the gray church tower,
Why, I wonder at your liking
    To wait for me half an hour.

I am sorry; what have you been doing
    All the while down here by the pool?
Do you hear that wild dove cooing?
    How nice it is here, and cool!

How that elder piles and masses
    Her great blooms snowy-sweet;
Do you see through the serried grasses
    The forget-me-nots at your feet?

And the fringe of flags that encloses
    The water; and how the place
Is alive with pink dog-roses
    Soft colored like your face?

You like them?—shall I pick one
    For a badge and coin of June?
They are lovely, but they prick one
    And they always fade so soon.

Here's a rose.   I think love like this is,
    That buds between two sighs,
And flowers between two kisses,
    And when it is gathered dies.

It is surely a grievous thing, love,
    That love should fade in one's sight;
It were better surely to fling love
    Off while the bloom is bright.

26

The frail life will not linger,
　　Best throw the rose away,
Though the thorns having scratched one's finger
　　Will hurt for half a day.

What, tears ? — you will keep it and see it
　　Fade and its petals fall ? —
If you will — why, Amen, so be it :
　　You may be right, after all.

J. B. B. NICHOLS

AN INTERLUDE

YOU taught me all that Love could be,
　　You filled my life with joy untold;
Could I give less than all to thee,
　　Or offer only dross for gold?

I brought my heart and laid it low,
　　For lifelong service at your feet;
The love of all my days I owe
　　To one who made my life so sweet.

But then there came another day,
　　The rhythm of the poem broke;
We said good-by, you went away;
　　The dream had ended — I awoke.

Ah, still within my heart you reign
　　And there none other shall intrude;
But you are fancy-free again
　　And I was but — an Interlude.

INDEED, they have not grieved me sore,
  Your faithlessness and your deceit;
The truth is, I was troubled more
  How I should make a good retreat:
Another way my heart now tends;
We can cry quits, and be good friends.

I found you far more lovable,
  Because your fickleness I saw,
For I myself am changeable
  And like, you know, to like doth draw:
Thus neither needs to make amends;
We can cry quits, and be good friends.

When I was monarch of your heart,
  My heart from you did never range;
But from my vassal did I part,
  When you your lady-love did change:
No penalty the change attends;
We can cry quits, and be good friends.

Farewell! We'll meet again some day,
  And all our fortunes we'll relate;
Of love let's have no more to say,
  'Tis clear we're not each other's fate.
Our game in pleasant fashion ends;
We can cry quits, and be good friends.

                         CATHERINE GRANT FURLEY

WHEN THOU ART NEAR

WHEN thou art near, the rose doth seem less fair,
    The lily pale is shorn of half its grace,
I only see the glory of thy hair,
  I only know the beauty of thy face,
Thy presence gladdens like the vernal year,
And it is always May when thou art near.

                        F. B. DOVETON

IF ONLY I MIGHT WRITE

MY dear, if only I might write,
    How many tender things I'd say —
The place seems empty of delight
  Since you have gone so far away;
I'd tell you how I oft recall
  Those fair, sweet pictures once we drew,
I'd tell you how I miss them all
  If only I might write to you.

If only I might write to you
  I'd tell you how reverse of gay,
How dull each place and person seems,
  And how I curse the lagging day
And bless night only for its dreams —
  I'd tell you how your voice still rings
Within my memory clear and true,
  I'd tell you — oh! a heap of things
If only I might write to you.

LOVE'S A RIDDLE

THE flame of love assuages,
 When once it is revealed;
But fiercer still it rages
 The more it is concealed.
Consenting makes it colder;
 When met it will retreat:
Repulses make it bolder,
 And dangers make it sweet.

HENRY CAREY

UNSATISFACTORY

"HAVE other lovers — say, my love, —
 Loved thus before to-day?" —
  "*They may have, yes! they may, my love;*
  Not long ago they may."

" But though they worshipped thee, my love,
Thy maiden heart was free?"
  "*Don't ask too much of me, my love;*
  Don't ask too much of me!"

" Yet now 'tis you and I, my love,
Love's wings no more will fly?"
  "*If love could never die, my love*
  Our love should never die."

" For shame! and is this so, my love,
And Love and I must go?" —
  "*Indeed I do not know, my love,*
  My life, I do not know."

" You will, you must be true, my love,
Nor look, nor love anew ! " —
  " *I'll see what I can do, my love,*
  I'll see what I can do."

FREDERICK W. H. MYERS

HER EYES

WHEN the little stars are shining
    In the azure skies
They are like the lights reclining
  In my darling's eyes ;
They are jealous and are keeping
  All the day from sight,
But they venture when she's sleeping
  To adorn the night.

" VIOLA "

LOVE THEE

I LOVE thee — I love thee !
    'Tis all that I can say ;
It is my vision in the night,
My dreaming in the day ;
The very echo of my heart,
The blessing when I pray :
I love thee — I love thee !
Is all that I can say.

THOMAS HOOD

WITH thee my thoughts are calm and sweet,
  Without thee they are wild and sad;
With thee my life is all complete,
  Without thee it is stormy — mad.
      Be true to me, my love, be true!
      I'm nothing, if I have not you.

With thee my heart is aye at rest,
  Without thee it is tempest-tost;
With thee my life is fully blest,
  Without thee I am wrecked and lost.
      Be true to me, my love, be true!
      I'm nothing if I have not you.

MARY COWDEN CLARKE

WHAT SOME ONE SAID

WHY should I not look happy,
  The world is all so bright?
For Some One said he loved me;
  He told me so last night.

Such words of love he whispered,
  I felt my blushes rise;
But half (he said) he told not,
  The rest was in his eyes.

He said to watch and guard me
  Would be his tenderest care;
If I am but beside him,
  Joy will be everywhere.

32

If love will make life lovely
Mine will be very sweet,
His love will strew with flowers
The path beneath my feet.

Then should I not be happy,
The world is all so bright?
For Some One said he loved me;
He told me so last night.

LOVE'S LANGUAGE

LOVE has a language that mocks at rules,
A foolish tongue that is all his own ;
Its words have values unknown to schools —
Dear for the sake of a look or a tone.
Learned it is not, nor is it wise
Yet it has purport earnest and true,
Full of such playful metonymies!
Figures — known to but Love and two ;
Gay ellipses — that leave to the guess
Tender half meanings ; metaphor bold,
Fond hyperbole — saying far less
Than the kind eyes tell, or the heart doth hold ;
Strange pet-names that are nouns unknown,
Epithets — mocking the love-charmed ears,
Verbs — that have *roots* in the heart alone,
Jests — that fill fond eyes with tears.

COUNTESS OF GIFFORD

DO I LOVE THEE

DO I love thee? Ask the bee
     If she loves the flowery lea,
Where the honeysuckle blows
And the fragrant clover grows.
     As she answers, yes or no,
     Darling, take my answer so.

Do I love thee? Ask the bird
When her matin song is heard,
If she loves the sky so fair,
Fleecy cloud and liquid air.
     As she answers, yes or no.
     Darling, take my answer so.

Do I love thee? Ask the flower
If she loves the vernal shower,
Or the kisses of the sun,
Or the dew when day is done.
     As she answers, yes or no,
     Darling, take my answer so.

JOHN GODFREY SAXE

IF THE HEART BE TRUE

ALL things can never go badly wrong,
     If the heart be true and the love be strong;
For the mist, if it comes, and the weeping rain
Will be changed by love into sunshine again.

GEORGE MACDONALD

LOVE'S COURSE

A FLIGHT of fancy like a gleam
  Of sunlight over silken hair —
A chord of subtle sympathy
That stirs emotions pure as prayer. —
An aspiration and a joy
That makes the lowliest a king. —
A kiss — and all the universe
Encircled by a wedding ring!

MARY BERRI CHAPMAN

I WANT YOU

I WANT you — Oh! I want you, now and ever!
  Had I a million tongues, they could but cry
" I want you." All the hunger of my life
Speaks in these words. . . .

* * * * * *

It is a fearful thing
To love as I love thee ; to feel the world —
The bright, the beautiful, joy-giving world —
A blank without thee.

* * * * * *

Belovèd, at thy touch the entire bliss
Of being floods me ; in my heart straightway
Songs rise and gush and murmur without end.

IF thou wert only, love, a tiny flower,
  And I a butterfly with gaudy wings,
Flitting to changing scenes each changing hour,
  Careless of aught save that which pleasure brings —
Not even I could leave the lowliest glade
That held thy loveliness within its shade.

If thou wert but a streamlet in the vale,
  And I a sailor on a stormy sea,
Flying through whirling foam beneath the gale,
  Chartless in all that wild immensity —
Thy murmuring voice would echo in my soul
Through howling storm or crashing thunder-roll.

If, darling, thou wert but a far-off star,
  And I a weary wanderer o'er the plain,
Unwitting of celestial worlds afar,
  And knowing naught of all the shining train —
My glance would single out thy ray serene,
Though blazing suns and planets rolled between.

Yet, dear one, thou art these to me and more:
  My flower whose radiance passeth all decay;
My streamlet of sweet thoughts in endless store;
  My star to guide my steps to perfect day;
My hope in earth's dark dungeon of despair;
My refuge 'mid life's weary noonday glare.

H. ERNEST NICHOL

LOVE ME IF I LIVE

LOVE me if I live;
   Love me if I die;
What to me is life or death,
So that thou be nigh?

Once I loved thee rich,
Now I love thee poor;
Ah! what is there I could not
For thy sake endure?

Kiss me for my love!
Pay me for thy pain!
Come! and murmur in my ear
How thou lov'st, again.
"BARRY CORNWALL"

I LOVE THEE

I LOVE thee as the flow'rets fair
   Love sunbeams on the lea;
I love thee as the birds of air
   Love dawning spring to see;
I love thee as the rippling stream
   Loves wending to the shore;
I love thee when awake, a-dream,
   Oh could I love thee more.
JOHN OXENFORD

NOT violets I gave my love,
   That in their life are sweet and rare,
And deep in color, as the heart
   Whose every thought of her is prayer;
For violets grow pale and dry,
And lose the semblance of her eye.

No lily buds I gave my love,
   Though she is white and pure as they;
For they are cold to smell and touch,
   And blossom but a single day;
And pressed by love, in love's own page,
They yellow into early age.

But cyclamen I chose to give,
   Whose pale white blossom at the tips
(All else as driven snow) are pink,
   And mind me of her perfect lips;
Still, till this flower is kept and old
Its worth to love is yet untold.

Old, kept, and kissed, it does not lose
   As other flowers the hues they wear;
Love is triumphant, and this bloom
   Will never whiten from despair;
Rather it deepens as it lies,
This flower that purples when it dies.

So shall my love, as years roll by,
    Take kingly colors for its own;
Sole master of her vanquished heart,
    Am I not master of a throne?
Crushed by no foot, nor cast away,
My purple love shall rule the day.

C. C. FRAZER-TYTLER

O LOVE, IF LIFE SHOULD BE

O LOVE, if life should be
    Merely the golden key
To love more vast —   .
If there should be a place
    Where spirits can embrace
        And kisses last.

*   *   *   *   *   *

O love! O fire! once he drew
With one long kiss my whole soul through
My lips, as sunlight drinketh dew.

NO ONE ELSE IS YOU

SO many are more beautiful?
    Sweetheart, that may be true!
So many are much better? —yes,
    But no one else is "you."

I THINK OF THEE

I THINK of thee
  When nightingales'
Sweet songs pervade
The leafy glade —
When are thy thoughts of me?

I think of thee
  Where twilight folds
Her evening wings
By shady springs —
Where are thy thoughts of me?

I think of thee
  With strange, sweet pain,
With longing fear,
With burning tear —
How are thy thoughts of me?
        From the German of Matthisson

LOVE

LOVE is not made of kisses, or of sighs,
Of clinging hands, or of the sorceries
And subtle witchcraft of alluring eyes.

Love is not made of broken whispers ; no!
Nor of the blushing cheek, whose answering glow
Tells that the ear has heard the accents low.

Love is not made of tears, nor yet of smiles ;
Of quivering lips, or of enticing wiles ;
Love is not tempted ; he himself beguiles.

This is Love's language, but this is not Love.

If we know aught of Love, now shall we dare
To say that this is Love, when well aware
That these are common things, and Love is rare.

As separate streams may, blending, ever roll
In course united, so, of soul to soul,
Love is the union into one sweet whole.

As molten metals mingle ; as a chord
Swells sweet in harmony ; when Love is lord,
Two hearts are one, as letters form one word.

One heart, one mind, one soul, and one desire,
A kindred fancy, and a sister fire
Of thought and passion ; these can Love inspire.

This makes a heaven of earth ; for this is Love.

BECAUSE YOU LOVE ME, DEAR

DEAR heart, life's storms around us beat,
  The snares of sin around us meet,
But love has made the bitter sweet,
  And seems to banish fear;
And though my way is fraught with pain,
A wondrous courage I maintain,
  Because you love me, dear.

Not much I heed cruel scandal's sting,
But if, perchance, distress it bring,
Your tender care is everything,
  And brighter hopes appear;
And when the hours of day have flown
You more and more become my own,
  Because you love me, dear.

And when for tears I cannot see,
When tempted, dear, I look to thee,
Then all the sinful shadows flee
  And soon the sky grows clear —
Oh precious love, oh priceless boon,
Our longing souls may now commune,
  Because you love me, dear.

"VIOLA"

EPIGRAM

WHEN first my true love crown'd me with her smile,
  Methought that Heaven encircled me the while!
When first my true love to mine arms was given,
Ah, then methought that I encircled Heaven.

GERALD MASSEY

LIFE WITHOUT LOVE

LIFE without love is like
  Day without sunshine,
Roses bereft of
  Sweet nature's perfume;
Love is the guide mark
To those who are weary
Of waiting and watching
  In darkness and gloom.

Love to the heart is like
Dewdrops to violets
Left on the dust-ridden
  Roadside to die;
Love leads the way
To our highest endeavors,
Lightens and lessens
  The pain of each sigh.

Life without love
Is like spring without flowers,
Brook streams that move not
  Or star-bereft sky.
Love creates efforts
Most worthy and noble,
Prompts us to live
  And resigns us to die.

SONG

WHEN stars are in the quiet skies,
  Then most I pine for thee;
Bend on me then thy tender eyes
  As stars look on the sea!
For thoughts, like waves that glide by night,
  Are stillest when they shine.
Mine earthly love lies hushed in light
  Beneath the heaven of thine.

LORD LYTTON

II

LOVE'S NOONTIDE

Love rules the court, the camp, the grove,
And men below, and saints above,
For love is heaven, and heaven is love.

SIR WALTER SCOTT

Mysterious love, uncertain treasure.
Hast thou more of pain or pleasure ?
Endless torments dwell about thee :
Yet who would live and live without thee !

JOSEPH ADDISON

Put thou thy trust in those who love ;
In no false heart may love abide.

FOR LOVE'S SWEET SAKE

BECAUSE you have no golden hoard,
   Or broad and fertile lands to show,
Or wealth in glittering caskets stored,
   You fear to whisper — what I know.
You think 'twould be a grievous wrong
   Me from my smoother paths to take,
Nor understand how brave and strong
   My heart could be for love's sweet sake.

Because you are a man, you seek
   To hide the tender pain you feel ;
And I, a woman, should not speak
   One word your secret wound to heal ;
Yet, knowing well that each for each
   Life's fullest harmonies could wake,
I fain would place within your reach
   The gift of love for love's sweet sake.

Because the ways you tread are rough,
   Shall we two always stand apart ?
Nay, let me own 'twould be enough
   To share your weal and woe, dear heart!
If you must bear a daily cross,
   Why, I will half the burden take ;
And what you choose to call my loss,
   Count truest gain for love's sweet sake.

E. MATHESON

UNLESS

UNLESS you can think when the song is done,
   No other is soft in the rhythm ;
Unless you can feel, when left by One,
   That all men else go with him ;
Unless you can know, when unpraised by his breath,
   That your beauty itself wants proving,
Unless you can swear, " For life, for death!" —
   Oh, fear to call it loving!

Unless you can muse in the crowd all day,
   On the absent face that fixed you ;
Unless you can love, as the angels may
   With the breadth of heaven betwixt you ;
Unless you can dream that his faith is fast
   Through behooving and unbehooving,
Unless you can *die* when the dream is past
   Oh, never call it loving.

Mrs. E. B. Browning

HOW LOVE COMES

*   *   *   *   *   *

L IKE Dian's kiss, unasked, unsought,
   Love gives itself, but is not bought;
  Nor voice, nor sound betrays
  Its deep, impassioned gaze.

It comes, — the beautiful, the free
The crown of all humanity, —
  In silence and alone
  To seek the elected one.

It lifts the boughs whose shadows deep
Are Life's oblivion, the Soul's sleep,
  And kisses the closed eyes
  Of him, who slumbering lies.

O weary hearts!   O slumbering eyes!
O drooping souls whose destinies
  Are fraught with fear and pain,
  Ye shall be loved again!

No one is so accursed by fate,
No one so utterly desolate,
  But some heart, though unknown
  Responds unto his own.

Responds, — as if with unseen wings
An angel touched its quivering strings
  And whispers, in its song,
  "Where hast thou stayed so long?"

          H. W. LONGFELLOW

51

A YEAR ago, a year ago,
  I thought my heart was cold and still,
That love it never more could know,
  That withering time and sorrow's chill
Had frozen all its earlier glow, —
A year ago, a year ago,
I said, " I ne'er shall love again ; "
But ah ! I had not *seen thee*, then.

A year ago, a year ago,
  My soul was wrapt in grief and gloom,
And sighs would swell and tears would flow
  As, bending o'er the lost one's tomb
I thought of her who slept below, —
A year ago, a year ago,
I felt I ne'er could love again ;
But ah! I had not *known thee*, then.

A year ago, a year ago,
  All vain were beauty's witching wiles,
And eye of light, and breast of snow,
  And raven tress, and lip of smiles, —
They could not chase the rooted woe,
A year ago, a year ago,
I never wished to love again
But ah! I had not *kissed thee*, then.

Lord Strangford

A S the flight of a river
     That flows to the sea,
My soul rushes ever
   In tumult to thee.

A twofold existence
   I am where thou art;
My heart in the distance
   Beats close to thy heart.

Look up, I am near thee,
   I gaze on thy face;
I see thee; I hear thee;
   I feel thine embrace.

*   *   *   *   *   *

Oh, all that I care for,
   And all that I know,
Is that without wherefore,
   I worship thee so.

As through the stone breaketh
   A tree to the ray,
As a dreamer forsaketh
   The grief of the day,

My soul in its fever
   Escapes unto thee;
O dream to the griever,
   O light to the tree!

A twofold existence
I am where thou art;
Hark, hear in the distance
The beat of my heart!
LORD LYTTON

THE ROSARY

THE hours I spent with thee, dear heart,
Are as a string of pearls to me;
I count them over, every one apart,
My rosary.

Each hour a pearl, each pearl a prayer,
To still a heart in absence wrung;
I tell each bead until the end, and there
A cross is hung.

Oh, memories that bless — and burn!
Oh, barren gain — and bitter loss!
I kiss each bead and strive at last to learn,
To kiss the cross,
Sweetheart,
To kiss the cross.
ROBERT CAMERON ROGERS

A WOMAN'S QUESTION

BEFORE I trust my fate to thee,
Or place my hand in thine,
Before I let thy future give
Color and form to mine, —
Before I peril all for thee, question thy soul to-night,
for me.

54

I break all slighter bonds, nor feel
  One shadow of regret:
Is there one link within the past
  That holds thy spirit yet?
Or is thy faith as clear and free as that which I can
    pledge to thee?

Does there within thy dimmest dreams
  A possible future shine,
Wherein thy life could henceforth breathe
  Untouched, unshared by mine?
If so, at any pain or cost, O tell me before all is
    lost!

Look deeper still.   If thou canst feel
  Within thy inmost soul
That thou hast kept a portion back,
  While I have staked the whole,
Let no false pity spare the blow, but, in true mercy,
    tell me so.

Is there within thy heart a need
  That mine cannot fulfil?
One chord that any other hand
  Could better wake or still?
Speak now, lest at some future day, my whole life
    wither and decay.

Lives there, within thy nature hid,
  The demon-spirit. Change,
Shedding a passing glory still,
  On all things new and strange?
It may not by thy fault alone, but shield my heart
    against thy own.

Couldst thou withdraw thy hand one day,
 And answer to my claim
That fate, and that to-day's mistake,
 Not thou, had been to blame?
Some soothe their conscience thus; but thou — O,
 surely thou wilt warn me now!

ADELAIDE ANNE PROCTER

PARTING

TOO fair, I may not call thee mine,
 Too dear, I may not see
Those eyes with bridal beacons shine;
 Yet, darling. keep for me —
Empty and hush'd, and safe apart —
 One little corner of thy heart.

Thou wilt be happy, dear ! and bless
 Thee, happy may'st thou be.
I would not make thy pleasure less;
 Yet, darling, keep for we —
My life to light, my lot to leaven —
 One little corner of thy Heaven.

Good-by, dear heart ! I go to dwell
 A weary way from thee;
Our first kiss is our last farewell,
 Yet, darling, keep for me —
Who wander outside in the night —
 One little corner of thy light.

GERALD MASSEY

TWO TRUTHS

"DARLING," he said, "I never meant
  To hurt you;" and his eyes were wet.
"I would not hurt you for the world;
  Am I to blame if I forget?"

"Forgive my foolish tears!" she cried,
  "Forgive! I knew that it was not
Because you meant to hurt me, Sweet, —
  I knew it was that you forgot!"

But all the same, deep in her heart
  Rankled this thought, and rankles yet:
When love is at its best, one loves
  So much that he cannot forget.

HELEN HUNT JACKSON

SONG

WE must love, and unlove, and, it may be,
  Live into and out of anon
Lovetimes no few in a lifetime,
  Ere lifetime and lovetime be one.
For to love it is hard, and 'tis harder
  Perchance to be loved again.
But if living be not loving
  Then living is all in vain.

OWEN MEREDITH

YOU KISSED ME

YOU kissed me! My head had drooped low on your
    breast,
With a feeling of shelter and infinite rest;
And a holy emotion my tongue dared not speak
Flashed up in a flame from my heart to my cheek.
Your arms held me fast. Oh, your arms were so bold!
Heart beat against heart in their passionate fold;
Your glances seemed drawing my soul through my eyes
As the sun draws the mist from the seas to the skies;
And your lips clung to mine till I prayed in my bliss,
They might never unclasp from that rapturous kiss.

You kissed me! My heart and my breath and my will,
In delicious joy for the moment stood still;
Life had for me then no temptations, no charms,
No vista of pleasure outside of your arms;
And were I this instant an angel possessed
Of the peace and the joy that are given the blest,
I would fling my white robes unrepiningly down,
And tear from my forehead its beautiful crown
To nestle once more in that haven of rest,
Your lips upon mine, my head on your breast.

You kissed me! My soul in a bliss so divine
Reeled and swooned like a drunken man foolish with
    wine;
And I thought 'twere delicious to die then, if death
Could but come while my lips were yet moist with your
    breath;

'Twere delicious to die if my heart might grow cold
While your arms clasped me round in that passionate
    fold!
And these are the questions I ask day and night:
Must my life taste but once such exquisite delight?
Would you care if your breast were my shelter as then?
And if you were here would you kiss me again?

JOSEPHINE HUNT

SONNET

I SAW her once, once only, long ago;
  Yet now she often comes to me by night,
Known by her hair, so silken-soft and bright,
That veils warm cheeks where crimson roses throw
A tender flush o'er pallid lily-snow.
She speaks not; only her golden head is light
Above my heart, that throbs with wild delight —
Dreaming she takes the love she cannot know.

Dear distant love, doth some sweet spirit voice
Breathe in thine ear, when slumber is most deep,
All I were fain to tell if we should meet?
And dost thou come, because the word is sweet,
By shadowy paths we tread not save in sleep,
To bid me trust the future and rejoice?

IF I could have my dearest wish fulfilled,
  And take my choice of all earth's treasures too,
And ask from Heaven whatsoe'er I willed,
    I'd ask for you.

No man I'd envy, neither low nor high,
  Nor king in castle old or palace new;
I'd hold Golconda's mines less rich than I,
    If I had you.

Toil and privation, poverty and care,
  Undaunted I'd defy, nor future woo;
Having my wife, no jewels else I'd wear,
    If she were you.

Little I'd care how lovely she might be,
  How graced with every charm, how fond, how true:
E'en though perfection, she'd be naught to me
    Were she not you.

There is more charm for my true loving heart
  In everything you think, or say, or do,
Than all the joys of Heaven could e'er impart,
    Because it's you.

THOUGH OFT DECEIVED

SO, after all, 'tis better that we err
  In loving overmuch, though oft deceived,
Than make our heart a sealèd sepulchre
  From which the angel turns away aggrieved.

HER ANSWER

IF you could pluck earth's emerald
    And set it in a ring
To glorify my finger—
    I could not call you King!

If you could trap the planets
    And bind them in a crown
To magnify my glory—
    I should but cast it down!

But more than earth or heaven
    I'll hold my heart above,
If you will mould your passion
    To daily deeds of love.

                    MARY BERRI CHAPMAN

GIFTS

YOU ask me what — since we must part —
    You shall bring back to me.
Bring back a pure and faithful heart
    As true as mine to thee.

You talk of gems from foreign lands,
    Of treasure, spoil, and prize.
Ah love! I shall not search your hands
    But look into your eyes.

                    JULIANA HORATIA EWING

YOU are all I have to live for,
  All that I want to love,
All that the whole world holds for me
  Of faith in the world above.
You came — and it seemed too mighty
  For my human heart to hold,
It seemed in its sacred glory
  Like a glimpse thro' the gates of gold;
Like a life in its primal Eden,
  Created and formed anew —
This charm of a perfect manhood
  That I realize in you.

God created me a woman
  With a nature just and true
As the blue eternal ocean,
  As the heavens over you;
And you are mine till your Maker calls you,
  Your soul and your body, Sweet!
Your breath and the whole of your being
  From your kingly head to your feet;
Your eyes and the light that is in them,
  Your lips with their maddening wine,
Your arms with their passionate clasp, my King,
  Your body and soul are mine!

No power whatsoever,
  No will but God's alone,
Can take you from my keeping,
  You are His and mine alone.
I know not when, if ever,

I know not where, or how,
Death's hand may try the fetters
    That bind me here and now;
But some day when God beckons
    Where rise His fronded palms,
My soul shall cross the river
    And lay you in His arms; —
Forever and forever
    Beyond the silent sea,
You will rest in the Arms Eternal
    And still belong to me!

SHE LOVES AND LOVES FOREVER

OH! say not woman's love is bought
    With vain and empty treasure.
Oh! say not woman's heart is caught
    By every idle pleasure.
When first her gentle bosom knows
    Love's flame, it wanders never;
Deep in her heart the passion glows, —
    She loves and loves forever.

Oh! say not woman's false as fair,
    That like the bee she ranges;
Still seeking flowers more sweet and rare
    As fickle fancy changes.
Ah no! the love that first can warm
    Will leave her bosom never;
No second passion e'er can charm,
    She loves and loves forever.

Thomas Love Peacock

TO LOVE THERE IS NO END

THERE is an end to kisses and to sighs,
  There is an end to laughter and to tears:
An end to fair things that delight our eyes,
  An end to pleasant sounds that charm our ears,
An end to enmity's foul libelling,
  And to the gracious praise of tender friend;
There is an end to all but one sweet thing —
  To Love there is no end.

That warrior carved an empire with his sword,
  The empire now is but like him — a name;
That statesman spoke, and by a burning word
  Kindled a nation's heart into a flame;
Now naught is left but ashes, and we bring
  Our homage to new men; to them we bend.
There is an end to all but one sweet thing —
  To Love there is no end.

All beauty fades away, or else, alas!
  Our eyes grow dim and they no beauty see;
The pageantries of Nature pass and pass,
  Quickly they come and quickly do they flee;
And he who hears the voice of welcoming
  Hears next the slow, sad farewell of his friend;
There is an end to all but one sweet thing —
  To Love there is no end.

LOST LOVE

WHO wins his love shall lose her,
   Who loses her shall gain,
For still the spirit woos her,
   A soul without a stain;
And memory still pursues her
   With longings not in vain!

He loses her who gains her,
   Who watches day by day
The dust of time that stains her,
   The griefs that leave her gray,
The flesh that yet enchains her,
   Whose grace hath passed away!

Oh, happier he who gains not
   The love some seem to gain;
The joy that custom stains not
   Shall still with him remain,
The loveliness that wanes not,
   The love that ne'er can wane.

He dreams she grows not older
   The lands of dream among,
Though all the world wax colder,
   Though all the songs be sung,
In dreams doth he behold her
   Still fair and kind and young.

ANDREW LANG

SOMEWHERE OR OTHER

SOMEWHERE or other there must surely be
    A face I have not seen, a voice not heard,
A heart which not yet — never yet — ah me!
    Made answer to my word.

Somewhere or other — maybe far away
    Across the marge where yonder sun doth set,
Is one whose hours like mine are tinged with gray
    Because we have not met.

Somewhere — oh, heart, my heart, it may be near
    With ever narrowing space betwixt us twain —
Life will re-blossom when I meet my dear,
    And earth grow sweet again.
            Adapted from CHRISTINA G. ROSSETTI

FROM THE PERSIAN

WERE I despised and desolate and poor,
    Mocked of my foes, forsaken of my kin,
If I should cry for pity at thy door,
    O love, I wonder wouldst thou let me in?

Ah, but if pain or sorrow or disgrace
    Came to thee, which God grant shall never be,
Sleepless to serve thee and to see thy face
    To my life's end were bliss enough for me.
                J. B. B. NICHOLS

LOVE

LOVE is a King and every heart a throne,
  Life lacks its purpose if Love reigns not there,
Nothing on earth shall last save Love alone,
Love stands between our world and dark despair
  And turns the cheerless night to morning fresh and
    fair.

To some Love comes with smiles, and glad are they,
To some he comes with tears and sighing breath,
To some as slowly as the dawning day,
To some he comes as swift as sudden death;
  In all, in all the slumbering heart he quickeneth.

A quiver of the voice — and love is born,
Within the eyes, upon the lips he plays,
Hand touches hand — and life is less forlorn,
A rose is given, and in its heart conveys
  A message tender sweet that brightens all our days.

In Heaven there is no fairer thing than Love,
Than Love there is on earth no sweeter thing,
It is to be desired all else above,
And welcome to the heart, though pain it bring —
  O leave me not for aye, O Love, my King, my King

G. H. WESTLEY

LOVE CANNOT DIE

WEEP not that we must part;
  Partings are short, eternity is long.
Life is but one brief stage
And they that say love ends with life are wrong.
  List to thy own heart's cry:
  Love cannot die!

What though so far away?
Thy thoughts are still with me, and with thee mine;
  And absence has no power
To lessen what by nature is divine.
  List to thine own heart's cry:
  Love cannot die!

Then weep no more, My Love;
Weeping but shows thy trust in me is small.
  Faith is by calmness proved;
For know this truth: thou canst not love at all
  Unless thine own heart cry:
  Love cannot die!

ME AND THEE

ONE unto his Belovéd came
  And knocked and called upon her name;
And from within a voice full sweet
That made his heart to music beat,
  Cried, "Who is there?"
    And low he made reply
    "Love, it is I."

And the voice spoke in chill despair,
" No room within this narrow hut
  For thee and me."
And lo, immutably,
The door was shut.

Then the sad lover fled away,
And wept and fasted night and day,
  In desert places making prayer,
Nor saw the kindly face of men ;
And after many days again
  To his Belovéd's door he came
  And knocked and called upon her name :
And from within a voice thereto
  Cried, "Who is there ? "
And he whom love had taught, replied,
" It is thyself ! " And lo,
The door was opened wide.

ELLICE HOPKINS, *from the Persian*

LOVE UNIVERSAL

THERE'S not a wild flower blossoming,
  Nor creature of the field or wood,
Nor bird of all the greening spring,
But knows love's tender mood.

And there is not a heart on earth
That loves, but shall be loved again :
Some other heart hath kindred birth
And feels the same sweet pain.

CONSTANCY IN ABSENCE

SOME day I think you will be glad to know
That I have ever kept you in my heart,
And that my love has ever deeper grown
In all the time that we have lived apart.

Some day when you have slipped away from care,
And idly fall to dreaming of the past,
And sadly think of all your life has missed —
Will you remember my true heart at last?

Or will it come to pass some dreary night —
After a day that has been hard to bear,
When you are weary, heartsick, and forlorn,
And there is none to comfort or to care;

That you will close your tiréd eyes and dream
Of tender kisses falling soft and light,
Of restful touches smoothing back your hair —
And sweet words spoken from your heart's delight.

Perhaps, then, you'll remember and be glad,
That I so long kept you in my heart,
And that your soul's true home will yet be there
Although we wander silently apart.

RENOUNCEMENT

I MUST not think of thee; and tired yet strong,
I shun the love that lurks in all delight —
The love of thee — and in the blue heavens' height,

And in the dearest passage of a song.
Oh just beyond the sweetest thoughts that throng
  This breast, the thought of thee waits hidden yet
    bright;
But it must never, never come in sight;
I must stop short of thee the whole day long.

But when sleep comes to close each difficult day,
When night gives pause to the long watch I keep,
And all my bonds I needs must loose apart,
Must doff my will as raiment laid away,—
  With the first dream that comes with the first sleep
I run, I run, I am gathered to thy heart.
ALICE MEYNELL

TO ——

TELL me your joy, that I may tune my life
  To echo the glad music of your own,
The changing melody, the sunny strife
  Of harmonies blent in one full sweet tone.
So shall the faithful shadow of my night
  Heighten your happy radiance of delight.

Tell me your sorrow, that I may disdain
  Mirth and rejoicing, banish all relief,
Save the sad ecstasy, the cruel gain
  Of being one with you, dear heart, in grief.
You did deny me love — have you no woe,
  No pain, to share with one who loves you so ?

DOUBT

SOMETIMES, my darling, I have suffered doubt,
Sometimes — when what you said or did seemed
   cold,
A hand more chill than Death's took sudden hold
Upon my heart, and all the sunny view
Grew dark, my darling, when I doubted you;

That was a longer night than ever drew
Its sable curtain o'er the western red;
I lived and yet I felt that I was dead.
I prayed that I might hate you, but in vain,
The prayer reproached me with a deeper pain.

Then I recalled your tenderness to me,
And vowed I still would cherish sweet belief;
Cast off the shadow of my doubt and grief,
Forget what eyes had seen or ears had heard,
And deem the motive kinder than the word.

'Twas well, for time's ordeal proved your love,
Beyond your weary words I learned to see
The daily effort bravely made for me;
My heart was blind, dear love, when doubting you,
For oh, you loved me better than I knew!

Alas, could we but see with clearer eyes,
Alas, could we but hear with keener ears,
We should have truer hearts, live better years,
And not regret too late the brave and true,
The hearts that loved us better than we knew.

MARY BERRI CHAPMAN

SWEETHEART

SWEETHEART, I have no hero's face
  To plead my passion's cause,
No knightly, no persuasive grace
  To win the world's applause.
What should I do — what can I be,
Sweetheart, to be beloved of thee ?

The waters play not in my life,
  Like fountains sparkling clear,
They rush not with the torrent's strife ;
  Mine is the deep, still mere,
Where one bright face, beloved by me,
Sweetheart, I still reflected see.

No buds of Spring, no tender shoots,
  No Summer flowers that fade,
Only the Autumn's mellow fruits
  Are mine.   Art thou afraid,
Sweetheart, to trust thy life to me,
Who would lay down my life for thee?

                              HAMILTON AÏDÉ

WHY ?

WHY are we bereft of all happiness, dearest ?
  So little would help us, so little would cheer.
The heaviest trials, the sorrows severest
Would only be blessings when shared with you, dear.

                              "VIOLA"

73

WE LOVE BUT FEW

OH, yes, we mean all kind words that we say
    To old friends and to new;
Yet doth this truth grow clearer day by day:
    We love but few.

We love! we love! What easy words to say
And sweet to hear,
When sunrise splendor brightens all the way,
    And far and near,

Are breath of flowers and carolling of birds
And bells that chime.
Our hearts are light; we do not weigh our words
    At morning time!

But when the matin music all is hushed,
And life's great load
Doth weigh us down, and thick with dust
    Doth grow the road,

Then do we say less often that we love,
The words have grown!
With pleading eyes we look to Christ above
    And clasp our own.

Their lives are bound to ours by mighty bands,
No mortal strait
Nor death himself, with his prevailing hands
    Can separate.

74

The world is wide and many friends are dear,
And friendships true;
Yet do these words read plainer year by year:
We love but few.

UNSPOKEN

AH, never doubt my love is true
That not in speech it flows,
For, dear, I cannot tell it you,
My heart no language knows;
And still can only yearn and ache
In silence though it break.

But not by any speech is known
The hidden lore of deep and height;
The sea has nothing but a moan,
The dark is silent and the light;
The grandest music needs no word
To make its meaning heard.

You dwell amidst my daily strife,
A thing apart, divine,
And all that's noblest in my life
Is incense at your shrine,
For every worthy deed I do
Is done for love of you.

A. ST. JOHN ADCOCK

PERSIAN LOVE SONG

A S the cloud to the wind I am docile to thee;
As the rose to the nightingale sweet would I be,
And deep in thy thought as a pearl in the sea.

Thou art gone — falls the dark ! Thou art here —
breaks the morn !
Our sunlight without thee seems brilliance forlorn;
And this world's a dead king, of all royalty shorn.

What is love but a bird that would touch the blue sky ?
What is love but a viol-string pitched far too high ?
What is love but the heart's unappeasable cry ?

I wait thee, heart's dearest — let life be the grove
Where I long for and meet thee, and walk with my
love —
The green lawns for carpet, the white stars above.

BLANCHE LINDSAY

WHEN WILL LOVE COME ?

S OME find Love late, some find him soon,
Some with the rose in May,
Some with the nightingale in June,
And some when skies are gray.

Love comes to some with smiling eyes,
And comes with tears to some;
For some Love sings, for some Love sighs,
For some Love's lips are dumb.

75

I WAIT THEE, HEART'S DEAREST

How will you come to me, fair Love?
  Will you come late or soon?
With sad or smiling skies above,
  By light of sun or moon?

Will you be sad, will you be sweet,
  Sing, sigh, love, or be dumb?
Will it be summer when we meet,
  Or autumn ere you come?

PAKENHAM BEATTY

SWEETHEART, GOOD-BY!

SWEETHEART, good-by! The fluttering sail
  Is spread to waft me far from thee,
And soon before the fav'ring gale
  My ship shall bound upon the sea.
Perchance all desolate and forlorn,
  These eyes shall miss thee many a year,
But unforgotten every charm —
  Though lost to sight, to memory dear.

Sweetheart, good-by! one last embrace!
  O cruel Fate, true souls to sever!
Yet in this heart's most sacred place
  Thou, thou alone shall dwell forever!
And still shall recollection trace
  In Fancy's mirror, ever near,
Each smile, each tear, that form, that face, —
  Though lost to sight, to memory dear.

JENKYN (about 1700)

WITH NO ONE TO LOVE US

SCENES that are brightest
  May charm us awhile;
Hearts that are lightest
  And eyes that smile;
Yet o'er them above us
  Though Nature beam,
With no one to love us
  How sad they seem.

EDWARD BALL

WILT THOU BE LONG?

WILT thou be long? The workful day is o'er,
  The wind croons softly to the sleeping sea;
At the old spot upon the lonely shore
    I wait for thee.
Home to his nest the swift gray gull is winging,
Through the still dusk I hear the sailor's song,
Night to the weary, rest from toil is bringing —
    Wilt thou be long?

Wilt thou be long? The darkness gathers fast,
  The daisies fold their fringes on the lea;
Time is so fleeting, and youth will not last,
    Oh, come to me!
In the clear west a silver star is burning,
But sad misgivings all my bosom throng,
With anxious heart I wait for thy returning —
    Wilt thou be long?

E. MATHESON

MAN'S LOVE

MAN'S love is of man's life a thing apart.
'Tis woman's whole existence: man may range
The court, camp, church, the vessel, and the mart;
  Sword, gown, gain, glory, offer in exchange,
Pride, fame, ambition, to fill up his heart,
  And few there are whom these cannot estrange;
Men have all these resources, we but one,
To love again, and be again undone.

BYRON

WHEN WE ARE PARTED

WHEN we are parted let me lie
    In some far corner of thy heart,
  Silent and from the world apart,
Like a forgotten melody:
Forgotten of the world beside,
  Cherished by one, and one alone
  For some loved memory of its own;
So let me in thy heart abide
    When we are parted.

When we are parted, keep for me
  The sacred stillness of the night;
  That hour, sweet Love, is mine by right:
Let others claim the day of thee!
The cold world sleeping at our feet,
  My spirit shall discourse with thine; —
  When stars upon thy pillow shine,
At thy heart's door I stand and beat
    Though we are parted.

HAMILTON AÏDE

WHEN SHE COMES

SOMETIMES I think I will be cold with her
       When next we meet, — and with indifferent
           words
I'll set a barrier 'twixt her heart and mine.
I'll speak of friendship — ah, how chill that word
Strikes on my ear after what we *have been*.
But then 'twere best; no more of love, no more! —
So will I greet her when we meet again.

But when she comes, ah! then within my heart
The fount of passion bursts these icy bounds.
I only hold my longing arms to her,
And gaze into her eyes, and kiss her hair,
And clasp her, clasp her to my yearning breast.

G. H. WESTLEY

LOVE ME NOT

LOVE me not for comely grace,
       For my pleasing eye or face,
Nor for any outward part:
No, nor for my loving heart!
For these may fail or turn to ill:
    So thou and I shall sever.
Keep therefore a true woman's eye,
And love me still, but know not why!
So hast thou the same reason still
    To dote upon me ever.

JOHN WILBYE (1609)

TO SIGH, YET FEEL NO PAIN

TO sigh, yet feel no pain;
　　To weep, yet scarce know why;
To sport an hour with beauty's chain,
　　Then throw it idly by;
To kneel at many a shrine,
　　Yet lay the heart on none;
To think all other charms divine,
　　But those we just have won;
This is love — careless love —
Such as kindleth hearts that rove.

To keep one sacred flame
　　Through life, unchill'd, unmov'd;
To love in wintry age the same
　　That first in youth we loved;
To feel that we adore
　　To such refined excess,
That though the heart would break with *more*,
　　We could not live with *less*;
This is love — faithful love, —
Such as saints might feel above.

THOMAS MOORE

THE UNSPOKEN QUESTION

I THOUGHT I must be dreaming
  The day you whispered low,
And told me the sweet secret
  That I alone must know.

I listened quite in silence,
  Perhaps you thought me cold;
My heart was overflowing
  With tenderness untold.

Just for one fleeting moment,
  One only did you stay.
Were you and I both dreaming
  That happy summer's day?

I DO NOT LOVE THEE

I DO not love thee! — no! I do not love thee!
  And yet when thou art absent I am sad;
And envy even the bright blue sky above thee,
Whose quiet stars may see thee and be glad.

I do not love thee! — yet, I know not why,
Whate'er thou dost seems still well done, to me —
And often in my solitude I sigh —
That those I *do* love are not more like thee!

I do not love thee! — yet, when thou art gone
I hate the sound (though those who speak be dear)
Which breaks the lingering echo of the tone
Thy voice of music leaves upon my ear.

I do not love thee ! — yet thy speaking eyes,
With their deep, bright, and most expressive blue —
Between me and the midnight heaven arise,
Oftener than any eyes I ever knew.

I *know* I do not love thee ! yet, alas !
Others will scarcely trust my candid heart ;
And oft I catch them smiling as they pass,
Because they see me gazing where thou art.

HON. MRS. NORTON

LOVE IS FOREVER

LOVE is forever — think no more
    You give and take your heart at will :
'Tis mine — or was not mine before ;
You never loved — or love me still !

You seem to hate — appeared to love.
But one was false ; choose which you will.
You hate?   Your love a lie has proved !
You loved?   Why then you love me still!

Then say no more your love is dead,
Nor death, nor hell. true love can kill.
Were it a dream, it might have fled,
But love, you loved, and love me still.

E. E. BRADFORD

WHY I LOVE THEE

NOT for the splendor of the brow that shines
    Upon me at this minute, love;
Not for the cunning ringlet that entwines
Snake-like the finger in it, love;
Not for thy wit, nor for thy radiant smiles,
Nor that sweet voice that my dark hour beguiles,
Do I adore thee ! But because I see
Something none other has, sweetheart, in thee.

There is a beauty that a man desires,
And wearies with possessing, love —
What is the secret charm that never tires ?
A secret worth the guessing, love !
And thou hast guessed it — of the stars and moon
And glad returning morn ; for I as soon
Of Nature's fairest sights and sounds could tire
As, kneeling here, could other shrine desire.

HAMILTON AÏDÉ

LOVE

LOVE is not a feeling to pass away,
    Like the balmy breath of a summer's day;
It is not — it cannot be — laid aside;
It is not a thing to forget or hide.
It clings to the heart — ah, woe is me ! —
As the ivy clings to the old oak tree.

CHARLES DICKENS

LIGHT

THE night has a thousand eyes,
 The day but one;
Yet the light of the bright world dies
 With the dying sun.

The mind has a thousand eyes,
 The heart but one;
Yet the light of the whole life dies
 When love is done.

F. W. BOURDILLON

LOVE'S WAKING

IS Love a dream?   In truth, they tell me so,
 And pity me because I cannot know
That tender glances, whispers sweet and low,
 Thrill for a summer's day and are no more.

But this I know, that if it is a dream,
I would not be as wise as they, to deem
That fair things can be false, and when they seem
 To promise most, that we should least adore.

They speak of waking from that dream, while I
Know but one waking, and that is not nigh.
For it will come when she I love shall die,
 Then I shall wake to sorrow evermore.

THE RECOMPENSE

I CALLED on Love and I said:
    I have eaten ashes for bread.
I have mingled my drink with tears
        All these years.

I have watched while others slept,
I have ofttimes fasted and wept,
I have taken no delight
        Day or night.

What hast thou done for me
Who have given my life to thee,
And have paid ceaseless vows
        In thy house?

I have humbled myself at thy feet,
And taken bitter for sweet,
And have striven to fulfil
        All thy will.

Hast thou brought me any nigher
To the end of my desire?
Or what guerdon hast thou given,
        Love, in heaven?

I am weak and thou art strong,
And thou hast proved me long;
What hast thou given, O Lord,
        For reward?

I cried upon Love and he heard
And he answered me but a word;
From the height of heaven above
Love said — "Love!"

UNTIL DEATH

MAKE me no vows of constancy, dear friend,
  To love me, though I die, thy whole life long,
And love no other till thy days shall end —
  Nay, it were rash and wrong.

If thou canst love another, be it so;
  I would not reach out of my quiet grave
To bind thy heart, if it should choose to go —
  Love should not be a slave.

My placid ghost, I trust, will walk serene
  In clearer light than gilds those earthly morns,
Above the jealousies and envies keen
  Which sow this life with thorns.

Thou wouldst not feel my shadowy caress,
  If, after death, my soul should linger here;
Men's hearts crave tangible, close tenderness,
  Love's presence warm and near.

It would not make me sleep more peacefully
  That thou wert wasting all thy life in woe
For my poor sake; what love thou hast for me
  Bestow it ere I go!

Carve not upon a stone when I am dead
　The praises which remorseful mourners give
To women's graves — a tardy recompense —
　But speak them while I live.

Heap not the heavy marble on my head
　To shut away the sunshine and the dew;
Let small blooms grow there, and let grasses wave,
　And raindrops filter through.

Thou wilt meet many fairer and more gay
　Than I; but, trust me, thou canst never find
One who will love and serve thee night and day
　With a more single mind.

Forget me when I die!　The violets
　Above my rest will blossom just as blue,
Nor miss my tears; e'en nature's self forgets,
　But while I live, be true!

TO MABEL

WITH leaden foot Time creeps along,
　　When thou, dear, art away.
With thee, nor plaintive was my song,
　Nor tedious was the day.

Ah! envious Time, my sentence change:
　Pass now with wingéd feet.
Fly swiftly when apart we range
　And loiter when we meet.

Adapted from RICHARD JAGO

LATE LOVE

LOVE came to me through the gloaming :
  The dew on his wings lay wet,
And the voice of his wistful greeting
  Was weary with old regret.
"O heart," he sighed at my casement,
  " Must I wait for a welcome yet ? "

He had come with the early flowers
  In the golden shining morn ;
But I asked a gift he bestowed not —
  A rose without a thorn.
So through the glare of the noontide,
  He left me to toil forlorn.

And now — in life's quiet evening
  When long are the shadows cast —
He comes with a few pale blossoms
  He has saved from a hungry past ;
And into my heart unquestioned
  I take him to rest at last.

M. E. MARTYN

IF THOU WERT FALSE

IF thou wert false to me, what could I do ? —
   If thou wert false to me what could I say ?
Could I look up and face the light of day —
      Thou faithless and I true ?

I could not dare to speak a word of blame,
   But in my heart the grief would lie and ache ;
Calmness without, my lips could never take
      The music of thy name.

The pain would choke me if I tried to weep —
   The stifled sorrow would lay waste within ;
Tears might relieve, but tears I might not win —
      Rest, but I could not sleep.

There could be neither tears, nor speech, nor rest,
   Till I forgave as I would be forgiven :
Then might the bonds of frozen grief be riven
      And sobbings ease my breast.

If thou wert false to me while I was true,
   I would remember rather than forget —
Loving thee still with that uncancelled debt
      Of love forever due.

                              ARTHUR L. SALMON

Alas for Love, if thou wert all,
   And naught beyond, O Earth !

                              FELICIA D. HEMANS

HAWTHORN

THE hand I love has dropped a spray
　Of softly-tinted, scented may,
　　The dew clings to it still;
The hand I love will never miss
The little flower that I can kiss
　　And fondle at my will.

The heart I love will never guess
What charm to soothe life's loneliness,
　　I found beside the way;
With hands close-clasped about my prize,
I walked beneath the tender skies
　　So tender yet so gray.

I walk alone, and I must go
Forever all my life below;
　　For me the gentle spring
That bears sweet messages to earth
Hath naught to say of joy's new birth
　　Or love's new blossoming.

And yet I love thee!　Well — 'tis well,
Though my poor lips may never tell
　　The tale with tender prayer.
I drop my poor heart in thy way,
As thou hast dropped this hawthorn spray,
　　But dost thou know — or care?

I hide thy flower upon a breast
That throbs with passionate unrest,
　　That aches and longs for thee!

But with calm face and placid eye
My poor, poor heart thou passest by,
　　And wilt not turn to see.

＊　　　＊　　　＊　　　＊　　　＊　　　＊

So be it — and so best!　My heart
Is fain to learn that selfless part,
　　The teaching is divine;
I love thee to life's longest day,
Though the dear hand that dropped the may,
　　Be never, never mine!

MY EARLY LOVE

MY early love!　I'll think on thee
　　When evening seeks its crimson throne;
Sweet hour, which gentle Memory
　　Delights to consecrate her own.
Ah! then thy cherished image clings
　　To all I meet, or hear, or see,
And twilight's breeze, like music brings
　　Thy voice of gladness back to me.

Friendship's young bloom may pass away
　　As dreams depart the sleeper's mind,
The hopes of life's maturer day
　　May fade and leave no trace behind;
But early love can never die,
　　The fairest bud of spring's bright years,
' Twill still look green in memory,
　　When time all other feeling sears.

YOU AND I

THE winter wind is wailing, sad and low,
  Across the lake and through the rustling sedge:
The splendor of the golden afterglow
  Gleams through the blackness of the great yew hedge;
And this I read on earth and in the sky:
We ought to be together, You and I.

Rapt through its rosy changes into dark,
  Fades all the west; and through the shadowy trees,
And in the silent uplands of the park,
  Creeps the soft sighing of the rising breeze.
It does but echo to my weary sigh,
We ought to be together, You and I.

My hand is lonely for your clasping, dear,
  My ear is tired, waiting for your call;
I want your strength to help, your laugh to cheer;
  Heart, soul, and senses need you, one and all.
I droop without your full frank sympathy;
We ought to be together, You and I.

We want each other so, to comprehend
  The dream, the hope, things planned, or seen, or
        wrought;
Companion, comforter, and guide, and friend
  As much as love asks love, does thought ask thought:
Life is so short, so fast the lone hours fly,
We ought to be together, You and I.

HENRY ALFORD

A LOVE LETTER

AND do you think of me
When you and I are far apart,
All day and every day, my heart,
Whatever you may do?
And do you with impatient pain,
Count all the days and all the hours,
Until that time of sun and flowers
When we shall meet again?

I lay the letter down —
Ah me ! my little childish love,
Life's April skies are blue above
    Thy path, and spring flowers crown
    The unbound beauties of thine hair;
Life's April daisies kiss thy feet,
Life's April song-birds clear and sweet
    Sing round thee everywhere.

All life is new to thee ;
Thy childish tasks are scarce set by,
Thy childish tears are hardly dry,
    Thy merry laugh rings free ;
    Love met thee suddenly one day
Among thy toys, he kissed thine eyes
And in the rush of sweet surprise
    The child soul slipped away.

Now love fills all thine heart,
It glorifies life's simple round,
It sets thee, robed, anointed, crowned,

And like a Queen, apart,
Above all common blame and praise —
Ah love! God giveth, giving thee,
The grace of vanished years to me,
   The joy of bygone days.

   Yet change the years have wrought;
I cannot count the days and hours,
Nor play, like thee, with daisy flowers
   At "loves me, loves me not;"
My heart and I are past our spring,
Youth's morning-prime, all rose and gold,
With pains and pleasures manifold,
   Life once, but once, doth bring.

   I love thee, little one,
With all the passion of my soul,
Firm as the fixed unchanging pole,
   And fervent as the sun;
   But, child, my life is not as thine,
The world must have her share of me,
I cannot sit at ease like thee
   Beneath love's spreading vine.

   I must be up and hold
My own in that unceasing strife
Whereby man wins his bread of life,
   His share of needful gold;
   I have my share to win and keep,
My share and thine to make a home
For thee and me in years to come —
   Ah love! true love lies deep!

I cannot count like thee
The hours and minutes as they fleet,
Nor loiter in the busy street
   As thou beside the sea
   To picture meetings far away ;
But I can love a lifetime long
With love that will be leal and strong,
   And green when life is gray.

I do not pause to tell
The minute beatings of my heart,
In crowded street and busy mart,
   Yet know I all is well:
   So like the heart within my breast
Thine image lies, and broods above
Its faithful pulses. Oh, my love,
   So sheltered, be at rest!

LOVE IS A TREE

LOVE is a tree that demands
   Culture and warmth at our hands ;
You who put ice to its root,
Look not thereafter for fruit.
              AUGUSTA DE GRUCHY

LOVE

PRAY, how comes Love?
   It comes unsought, unsent.
Pray, how goes Love?
   That was not Love that went.

THE MATCH OF LOVE

THE match of Love is of so quick a sort
    It can be lighted with the merest touch;
And let it once be kindled, e'en in sport,
Cool reason, thawing, finds the flame too much.
If Love within our hearts an entry gain,
Love is triumphant, all things else are vain.

LOVE'S FLAME

ALL thoughts, all passions, all delights,
    Whatever stirs this mortal frame,
Are but the ministers of Love,
And feed his sacred flame.

S. T. Coleridge

WHAT IT IS TO LOVE

IT is to be all bathed in tears;
    To live upon a smile for years;
To lie whole ages at a beauty's feet;
    To kneel, to languish, and implore;
    And still, though she disdain, adore: —
It is to do all this and think thy sufferings sweet.

    It is to gaze upon her eyes
    With eager joy and fond surprise;
Yet tempered with such chaste and awful fear,
    As wretches feel who wait their doom;
    Nor must one ruder thought presume,
Though but in whispers breathed, to meet her ear.

It is to hope, though hope were lost;
Though heaven and earth thy passion crossed;
Though she were bright as sainted queens above,
    And thou the least and meanest swain
    That folds his flocks upon the plain, —
Yet, if thou dost not hope, thou dost not love.

It is to quench thy joy in tears,
    To nurse strange doubts and groundless fears:
If pangs of jealousy thou hast not proved, —
    Though she were fonder and more true
    Than any nymph old poets drew, —
O never dream that thou hast loved!

If when the darling maid is gone,
Thou dost not seek to be alone,
Wrapped in a pleasing trance of tender woe,
    And muse and fold thy languid arms,
    Feeding thy fancy on her charms.
Thou dost not love, — for love is nourished so.

If any hopes thy bosom share
    But those which love has planted there,
Or any cares but his thy breast enthrall.
    Thou never yet his power hath known,
    Love sits on a despotic throne,
And reigns a tyrant, if he reigns at all.

Now if thou art so lost a thing,
    Here all thy tender sorrows bring,
And prove whose patience longest can endure;
    We'll strive whose fancy shall be lost

In dreams of fondest passion most,
For if thou thus hast loved, O never hope a cure !
Anna Letitia Barbauld

"LOVE, WITHOUT THEE"

AH, for this weary life !
    Were there not peace with thee —
Could I endure its strife,
    Did it not cease with thee?
Star of my dwelling-place,
    Where'er it be,
Earth would have lost its grace,
    Love, without thee !

Time robbeth, day by day,
    Bright hours of youth from us,
Yet he steals not away
    Constancy's truth from us.
Star ! that with Morning's light
    Shone over me,
How could I meet the Night,
    Love, without thee ?

Time, with unerring spade,
    Digs a grave low for us ;
Yet shall not love be laid
    There, when tears flow for us.
Star, that with purer beam
    Shines o'er Death's sea,
Joyless would heaven seem,
    Love, without thee !
Hamilton Aïdé

ONE ISN'T LOVED EVERY DAY

THE world is filled with folly and sin,
And Love must cling where it can, I say:
For Beauty is easy enough to win,
But one isn't loved every day.

OWEN MEREDITH

III

LOVE'S EVENING

Had we never loved so kindly,
Had we never loved so blindly,
Never met, or never parted,
We had ne'er been broken-hearted.

ROBERT BURNS

Love it begins with music and with song,
And ends with sorrow and with sighs ere long.

FROM THE TUSCAN

AWAKE

NO longer sleep,
    Oh, listen now.
I wait and weep,
    But where art thou?

Still barred thy door; the far east glows,
    The morning wind blows fresh and free;
Should not the hour that wakes the rose
    Awaken also thee?

All look for thee, Love, Light, and Song —
    Light in the sky deep red above,
Song, in the lark of pinions strong,
    And in my heart, true Love.

Apart we miss our nature's goal;
    Why strive to cheat our destinies?
Was not my love made for thy soul?
    Thy beauty for my eyes?

TORU DUTT

FATE

TWO shall be born the whole wide world apart,
   And speak in different tongues and have no thought
Each of the other's being, and no heed;
Yet these o'er unknown seas to unknown lands
Shall cross; escaping wreck, defying death,
And all unconsciously shape every act
And bend each wandering step unto this end,
That one day out of darkness they shall meet
And read life's meaning in each other's eyes.

And two shall walk some narrow way of life
So closely side by side, that should one turn
Ever so little space to left or right
They needs must stand acknowledged face to face;
Yet these with groping hands that never clasp,
With wistful eyes that never meet, and lips
Calling in vain on ears that never hear,
Shall wander all their weary days unknown
And die unsatisfied.   And this is Fate.

SUSAN MARR SPALDING

Copyright, 1892, by Roberts Bros.

AN APPEAL

AH! could you see me weep in anguish sore
   By the sad hearth I dare not call a home,
Sometimes I think, dear one. before my door
     Would you not come?

106

Could you but guess my joy when your eyes meet
   My wearied eyes in one divinest glance,
Up at my window you would look, my sweet,
     As if by chance.

If to my wounded heart you knew the balm
   Of sympathy, and love that has no guile,
Under my porch — a sister sweet and calm —
     You'd rest awhile.

Ah! darling, if you knew I loved, and how
   A love so great and pure your love must win,
Perhaps you'd lift the latch, — yes, even now, —
     And come within!

FLORENCE HENNIKER
after Sully Prudhomme

FORGIVE ME NOW

WAIT not the morrow, but forgive me now;
   Who knows what fate to-morrow's dawn may
  bring ?
Let us not part with shadow on thy brow,
   With my heart hungering.

Wait not to-morrow, but entwine thy hand
   In mine with sweet forgiveness full and free,
Of all life's joys I only understand
   This joy of loving thee.

Perhaps some day I may redeem the wrong,
   Repair the fault — I know not when or how.
O dearest, do not wait — it may be long —
   Only forgive me now.

MY darling, my darling, my darling,
   Do you know how I want you to-night?
The wind passes moaning and snarling,
   Like some evil ghost in its flight.
On the wet street your lamp's gleam shines redly:
   You are sitting alone — did you start
As I spoke?   Did you guess at the deadly
   Chill pain in my heart?

Out here the dull rain is falling,
   Just once — just a moment — I wait.
Did you hear the sad voice that was calling
   Your name, as I paused at the gate?
It was just a mere breath, ah, I know, dear,
   Not even Love's ears could have heard;
But oh! I was hankering so, dear,
   For one little word.

Do you think I am ever without you?
   Ever lose for an instant your face
Or the spell that breathes always about you,
   Of your subtle, ineffable grace?
Why, even to-night, put away, dear,
   From the light of your eyes though I stand,
I feel as I linger and pray, dear,
   The touch of your hand.

Ah me! for a word that could move you
   Like a whisper of magical art!
I love you! I love you! I love you!
   There is no other word in my heart.

Will your eyes that are loving, still love me?
  Will your heart, once so tender, forgive?
Ah! darling, stoop down from above me,
  And tell me to live.

BARTON GRAY

AFTER ALL!

I *THINK* that he loved me! at least, he said
  That the world could never be just the same,
After the ashes lay cold and dead,
  The ashes of love that were once aflame.
He said that always about my name,
  Was the sweet, sad sigh of an old regret!
That life could never be quite the same,
  Or quite as glad as of old — but yet —
I know that somewhere he lives — ah, me!
  Somewhere without me — beyond recall!
The old, sweet bondage has left him free —
                    After all!

I *know* that I loved him! at least. I know,
  That when the ashes were gray and dead,
I felt the flame of the long ago
  Brighten my life to a fiery red.
He was not worthy! Ah, so they said!
  Not worthy even an hour's regret!
So I told them the sweet old love was dead —
  Buried like other loves — but yet —
Could the waters of Lethe flow — ah, me!
  And cover the past beyond recall,
I know I could never again be free —
                    After all!

G. BUTT

PASSION AND PATIENCE

THE wine of life tastes stale and sour,
   The gilt comes off the golden year,
All shadowed is "each shining hour,"
   Because, sweetheart, you are not here.

The stupid people come and go,
   And prate of pleasures old and new;
But they offend and bore me so,
   Because, sweetheart, they are not you.

And you, meanwhile, accept what good
   The gods provide, and leave the rest;
Nor would you alter if you could
   The state of things that Fate thinks best:

For you — as happy days pass by
   And bring you friendships not a few —
May meet another Me; but I
   Shall never find another You.
        ELLEN THORNYCROFT FOWLER

AN UNEQUAL GAME

A MOMENT of loving and laughter,
   A jest and a gay good-bye.
If you in a short week after
   Forget, why may not I?

To you but a moment's feeling,
   A touch and a tender tone;
But a wound that knows no healing
   To me who am left alone.

THIS IS ALL

JUST a saunter in the twilight,
  Just a whisper in the hall,
Just a sail on sea or river,
Just a dance at rout or ball,
Just a glance that hearts enthrall —
This is all — and this is all.

Just a few harsh words of doubting,
Just a silence proud and cold,
Just a spiteful breath of slander,
Just a wrong that is not told,
Just a word beyond recall —
This is all — and this is all.

Just a life robbed of its brightness,
Just a heart by sorrow filled,
Just a faith that trusts no longer,
Just a love by doubting chilled,
Just a few hot tears that fall —
This is all — ah! this is all.

ROSE CHURCHILL

III

THE NOON OF LIFE

STAY one moment, ere you leave me;
  Having left me, time will show
You were thoughtless to deceive me,
  I was mad to love you so.
Though you say our lives must sever,
  Though I tell of broken ties,
You will hold me bound forever
  By your everlasting eyes.

You will find, *formosa cara*,
  If you take the pains to try,
Many a better man and far a
  Richer lover lord than I.
Though the past you try to smother,
  Saying truly we must part,
Dearest, you may find another,
  Never such a faithful heart.

Life may be a dark December
  Through the long approaching years;
When your folly I remember,
  My sad eyes will fill with tears.
You may drown my heart in sorrow,
  When my fancy sighs your name;
Break another heart to-morrow,
  I shall ever be the same.

When I dream of love mistaken,
  When the evening lamp is lit;
When I feel I am forsaken,
  When disconsolate I sit:

When the spring comes — then you met me —
   I may think it sad to live;
Your reproach is to forget me;
   My revenge is to forgive.

CLEMENT SCOTT

STRANGERS YET

STRANGERS yet!
   After years of life together,
After fair and stormy weather,
After travel in far lands,
After touch of wedded hands, —
Why thus joined?   Why ever met,
If they must be strangers yet?

   Strangers yet!
After strife for common ends,
After title of "old friends,"
After passions fierce and tender,
After cheerful self-surrender,
Hearts may beat and eyes be met
And the souls be strangers yet.

   Strangers yet!
Oh! the bitter thought to scan
All the loneliness of man : —
Nature by magnetic laws,
Circle unto circle draws,
But they only touch when met,
Never mingle — strangers yet.

LORD HOUGHTON

113

IF ONLY YOU WERE HERE

IF only you were here to-night;
　If I might lift my longing eyes to trace
Your dreamy eyes down-looking on my face,
With their half-veiled, half-smiling tenderness, —
O first and best and dearest, can you guess
How in my lonely heart your altar-flame
Would leap to sudden glorious fire, and shame
All these sad, darkened hours of fear and blame,
　　If only you were here ?

If only you were here to-night,
Here close beside me where the soft rain falls
And through the darkness the sweet church-bell calls,
And all the quiet world takes on repose, —
O warmest heart ! if you were here, so close
That I might lean down on your breast,
What could I ask of sweeter calm or rest ?
Who in God's happy world could be more blest
　　If only you were here ?

If only you were here to-night,
O Love, my Love, my Love, so far from me !
Through all dividing space, where'er you be,
My wingéd thoughts fly fast and far and free,
Seeking like birds to find their sheltering nest.
O gentle heart, make such a welcome guest !
Across the lonely world I know not where
I send the longing silence of this prayer —
　　If only you were here.

HESTER A. BENEDICT

114

DRIFTING AWAY

DRIFTING away from each other,
  Silently drifting apart;
Nothing between but the world's cold screen,
  Nothing to lose, but a heart.

Only two lives dividing
  More and more day by day;
Only one soul from another soul
  Steadily drifting away.

Only a man's heart striving
  Bitterly hard with its doom;
Only a hand, tender and bland,
  Slipping away in the gloom.

Nothing of doubt or wrong;
  Nothing that either can cure;
Nothing to shame; nothing to blame;
  Nothing to do, but endure.

The world cannot stand still,
  Tides ebb, and women change;
Nothing here that is worth a tear,
  One love less, nothing strange.

Drifting away from each other
  Steadily drifting apart;
No wrong to each that the world can reach,
  Nothing lost — but a heart!

                    BARTON GRAY

115

A REMONSTRANCE

DEEM, if thou wilt, that I am all, and worse
    Than all, they bid thee deem that I must be.
But ah ! wilt thou desert love's universe
    Deserting me?

Not for my sake be mine unworth forgiven,
   But for thine own.   Since I, despite my dearth
Of all that made thee what thou art, my Heaven,
    Am still thine Earth.

Who will hold dear the ashes of the days
   Burn'd out on altars deem'd no more divine?
Rests there of thy soul's wealth enough to raise
    A new god's shrine?

Who will forgive thy cheek its faded bloom
   Save he whose kisses that blanched rose hath fed?
Thine eyes, the stain of tears — save he for whom
    Those tears were shed?

Despite the blemisht beauty of thy brow,
   Thou wouldst be lonely couldst thou love again;
For love renews the beautiful.   But thou
    Hast only pain.

Ah, if thy heart can pardon yet, why yet
   Should not its latest pardon be for me?
And if thou *wilt not* pardon, canst thou set
    Thy future free?

*   *   *   *   *   *

Then if the flush of love's first faith be wan,
And thou wilt love again, again love me
For what I am — no saint, but still a man
That worships thee.

OWEN MEREDITH

WHEN LOVE SHALL COME

WHEN Love shall come —
Shall lay his torch upon your slumbering heart,
And as the fiery flames upleaping start
Wrap your whole soul in its effulgent glow —
When Love shall come to you, then you shall know,
You, who so scornfully my hand can slight,
The bitter anguish that is mine to-night.

Nay, do not jest !
Is it so small a thing, a strong man's love ?
So slight a thing to know that you can move,
Sway his whole being with your artless wiles.
Your madd'ning prodigality of smiles —
Is it so small a thing?   Nay, jest not so !
When Love shall come to you, then shall you know.

Oh, love of mine !
Half child, half woman !   In whose azure eyes
No touch of lovelight softly gleaming lies,
Some day you too before Love's feet will fall,
Your heart leap up to hear his clarion call
And in a flash reveal yourself new born —
God pity you if you should meet with scorn,
When Love shall come.

HAD I BUT KNOWN

HAD I but known, long years ago,
    The deep unrest, the weight of woe,
The pain of having loved you so !
    Had I but seen through mist of years
My bitter sacrifice of tears !

Had I but felt, as I do now,
    These scars of sorrow on my brow,
No seeds of promise had I sown,
    My life were not so weary grown,
        Had I but known.

                        CLEMENT SCOTT

GOOD-BYE

GOOD-BYE ! good-bye !   How hard to say
    When fondest hearts must sever !
One word, one look, thy hand in mine,
    And then we part forever.

Good-bye ! good-bye !   I hear it still,
    That bitter note of sadness,
Its lingering echoes sound to me
    A knell of dying gladness.

Good-bye ! good-bye !   Though sets the sun,
    Though falls the darkness coldly,
Remember thou hast duties yet,
    And face the future boldly.

Good-bye! good-bye! From out the past
   Looks forth thy face to cheer me;
Oh, do not ask me to forget,
   If Memory brings thee near me.

ABSENCE

WHAT shall I do with all the days and hours
   That must be counted ere I see thy face?
How shall I charm the interval that lowers
   Between this time and that sweet time of grace?

Shall I in slumber steep each weary sense,
   Weary with longing?— shall I flee away
Into past days, and with some fond pretence
   Cheat myself to forget the present day?

Shall love for thee lay on my soul the sin
   Of casting from me God's great gift of time;
Shall I these mists of memory locked within,
   Leave and forget life's purposes sublime?

Oh! how, or by what means, may I contrive
   To bring the hour that brings thee back more near?
How may I teach my drooping hope to live
   Until that blessed time, and thou art here?

I'll tell thee: for thy sake I will lay hold
   Of all good aims, and consecrate to thee,
In worthy deeds, each moment that is told
   While thou, belovéd one! art far from me.

For thee, I will arouse my thoughts to try
   All heavenward flights, all high and holy strains;
For thy dear sake I will walk patiently
   Through these long hours, nor call their minutes pains.

I will this dreary task of absence make
   A noble task-time, and will therein strive
To follow excellence, and to o'ertake
   More good than I have won, since yet I live.

So may this dooméd time build up in me
   A thousand graces which shall thus be thine;
So may my love and longing hallowed be,
   And thy dear thought an influence divine.

FRANCES ANNE KEMBLE

FRIENDS

LET us be friends: we may not now be more;
   Your silent glances make but poor amends
For all my pain. Speak as you did before—
   Let us be friends.

Love to my heart its fire no longer lends;
   'Tis chilled and hardened to its very core:
No quickening beat your presence now attends.

Yet would I not forget the joys of yore;
   And now that Fate has worked its cruel ends,
Shake hands and smile; for my sake, I implore,
   Let us be friends.

SAMUEL WOOD

LONGING

OH would that thou wert with me now, my own,
  For I so need thee, yearn thy voice to hear;
Would God my yearning, love, could bring thee near!
  Would that some gentle spirit heard my moan
And, touched to pity by its plaintive tone,
  Forth with my message laden, through the air
Sped swiftly, swiftly, fearing my despair —
Since I without thee, darling, am so lone —
And poured my longing in thy tender breast,
  So thou shouldst feel that I did need thee so,
Wouldst thou not give me pity, so distressed
  With burden of my loneliness and woe? —
Yea, thou wouldst fly to me, dear love, I know,
And in the knowing I am soothed and blessed.

G. H. WESTLEY

TOO LATE

THEY were together, — her eyes were wet,
  But her pride was strong and no tears would fall;
And he would not tell her he loved her yet,
  Though he yearned to forgive her all.

So now their lives are forever apart,
  She thinks: "Oh! had I but wept that day!"
And he, he asks of his lonely heart,
  "Ah! why did I turn away?"

From the Spanish of GUSTAVE BECQUER

AFTER MANY DAYS

IN autumn's silent twilight, sad and sweet,
  O love, no longer mine, alone I stand;
Listening, I seem to hear dear phantom feet
Pass by me down the golden wave-worn strand:
I think of things that were and things that be,
I hear the soft low ripples of the sea,
That to my thoughts responsive music beat.

And is it only five years since, O love,
That we in this old place stood side by side,
Where in the twilight once again I move?
Is this the same shore wash'd by the same tide?
My heart recalls the past a little space,
The sweet and the irrevocable days;
I knew not then how bitter life might prove.

I loved you then, and shall love till I die;
Your way of life is fair, it should be so,
And I am glad, though in dark years gone by
Hard thoughts of you I had; but now I know
A fairer and a softer path was meet
For treading of your dainty maiden feet:
Your life must blossom 'neath a summer sky.

*   *   *   *   *   *

And so I blame you not because you chose
A softer path of life than mine could be.
I keep our secret here, and no man knows

What passed five years ago 'twixt you and me —
Two loves begotten at the self-same time,
When that gold summertide was in its prime:
One love lives yet, and one died with the rose.
PHILIP BOURKE MARSTON

LOVE THAT AVAILETH

EASIER it were to give my life to thee,
    Its days of toil and hope, its utmost wealth;
To travel the wide earth, the pathless sea,
    Tending thy want, thy sickness, and thy health.

Such were a summer task, a soul's desire,
    Though I were bared of all things for thy sake.
There is a sacrifice whose worth is higher
    Than any gift supremest love can make.

To stand aside while others wait and tend thee —
    To know thee ministered by other care,
To watch while other loving hands defend thee —
    To see the service which I cannot share —

To joy when alien kindness is availing —
    To quench the jealous agony, the pain! —
O true heart's love, so patient, yet so failing,
    Such a high glory how canst thou attain?
ARTHUR L. SALMON

SHADOWS

YOU said, "I love you." Prodigal of sighs,
　　You said it o'er and o'er; I nothing said.
The lake lies still beneath the moonlit skies —
　　The water sleeps when stars shine overhead.

For this you blame me — but love is not less
　　Because its whisper is too faint to hear.
The sudden sweet alarm of happiness
　　Set seal upon my lips when you were near.

It had been best had you said less — I more:
　　Love's first steps falter and he folds his wings.
On empty nests the garish sun-rays pour —
　　Deep shadows fall around the brightest things.

To-day (how sadly in the chestnut tree
　　The faint leaves flutter and the cold wind sighs !) —
To-day you leave me, for you could not see
　　My soul beneath the silence of my eyes.

So be it, then ; we part ; the sun has set.
　　(Ah ! how that wind sighs ! how the dead leaves fall !)
Perhaps to-morrow whilst my cheek is wet,
　　You will have gay and careless smiles for all.

The sweet "I love you !" that must now go by
　　And be forgotten, breaks my heart to-day.
You said it, but you did not feel it — I
　　Felt it without a word that I could say.

C. E. MEETKERKE, after Victor Hugo

THE PRICE

JUST one kiss — two faces met
But the brows were knit and the cheeks were wet;
Just one kiss — then up and away;
But its mark will last for many a day.

Just one kiss, and just one word,
Softly spoken and hardly heard;
Just one word that was said through tears,
And told the story of all the years.

Just one look from the deep, dark eyes;
Just one grasp at a glorious prize;
Just one kiss — then up and away;
But ah! such a heavy debt to pay.

WALTER HERRIES POLLOCK

I KNOW that deep within your heart
   You hold me shrined apart from common things,
And that my step, my voice, can bring to you
   A gladness that no other presence brings.

And yet, dear love, throughout the weary days
   You never speak one word of tenderness,
Nor stroke my hair, nor softly clasp my hand
   Within your own in loving mute caress.

You think, perhaps, I should be all content
   To know so well the loving place I hold
Within your life, and so you do not dream
   How much I long to hear the story told.

You cannot know, when we two sit alone,
   And tranquil thoughts within your mind are stirred,
My heart is crying like a tired child
   For one fond look, one gentle, loving word.

Perhaps sometimes you breathe a secret prayer
   That choicest blessings unto me be given,
But if you say aloud, "God bless thee, dear,"
   I should not ask a greater boon from heaven.

'Tis not the boundless water ocean holds
   That gives refreshment to the thirsty flowers,
But just the drops that, rising to the skies,
   From thence descend in softly falling showers.

What matters that our granaries are filled
  With all the richest harvest's golden stores,
If we who own them cannot enter in,
  But famished, stand below the close-barred doors?

And so 'tis said that those who should be rich
  In that true love which crowns our earthly lot,
Go praying with white lips from day to day
  For love's sweet tokens, and receive them not.

THE SECRET

MY soul its secret has, my life too has its mystery,
    A love eternal in a moment's space conceived;
Hopeless the evil is, I have not told its history,
And she who was the cause, nor knew it nor believed.
Alas! I shall have passed close by her unperceived,
Forever at her side, and yet forever lonely,
I shall unto the end have made life's journey, only
Daring to ask for naught, and having naught received.

For her, though God has made her gentle and endearing,
She will go on her way distraught and without hearing
These murmurings of love that round her steps ascend;
Piously faithful still unto her austere duty,
Will say, when she shall read these lines full of her
    beauty,
" Who can this woman be?"— and will not comprehend.

H. W. LONGFELLOW,
From the French of Felix Arvers

127

DO YOU?

Do you feel sometimes in your dreaming
  The weight of my head on your breast?
Or the velvety touch of my kisses
  On your lips in passion impressed?

Do you hold me sometimes in your dreaming
  In a rapturous clasp on your heart?
Or cry in the depth of your yearning
  " 'Tis cruel to keep us apart? "

Does my hand with its lingering caresses
  Touch yours with its magic again
Till, starting, you wake from the pressure
  To find that your dreaming is vain?

Though light as the fall of a roseleaf,
  You'd feel the sweet weight of my kiss,
And. starting. you'd waken to kiss me,
  And taste love's ineffable bliss.

Ah! never again shall I see you,
  Nor look in your proud grand face,
Nor feel the sweet balm of your kisses,
  Or thrill to your tender embrace.

For our lives lie asunder forever,
  More wide than the cruel sea.
But I love you! I love you! I love you!
  And in dreams I will linger with thee.

FROM AFAR

GO thou thy way.   I do not seek to share
    The path which God hath girt with flowers for thee,
It lies before thee wrapped in sunshine fair,
    To know thee happy is enough for me.
If thou art safe and sheltered in the ark
    Of blessed home from earthly stress and strife,
It is enough for me, far off, to mark
    God's smile, and Love's, complete thy noble life.
It is enough for me to see thee share
    Life's banquet with thy dearest, crowned with flowers ;
No sigh of mine shall vex the scented air,
    No tear of mine shall mar thy happy hours.
I ask not for the children's bread, nor crumb
Cast to the dog, whose love, like mine, is dumb !

I ask for nothing, dear, but this — but this —
    Free leave to love thee all my lone life through ;
But if God set a limit to thy bliss,
    And change joy's roses to grief's bitter rue,
Then give me leave to whisper in thine ear
    Of love that lingers in a faithful heart,
That holds thee, lorn and lonely, dearest — dear ;
    Of love, whose idol and whose crown thou art !
Nay, nay, I dream !   Shall I forecast for thee
    Tears and a stricken heart ?   Now, God forbid !
I love thee, dear.   It is enough for me —
    What lies within the solemn future hid,
Who knows ?   I know whate'er the years bring round
To thee and me, love will be faithful found !

THE LAST TALK

COME out in the garden and walk with me,
    While the dancers whirl to that dreary tune ;
See.! the moonlight silvers the sleeping sea,
    And the world is as fair as a night in June.
Let me hold your hand as I used to do —
    This is the last, last time, you know,
For to-morrow a wooer comes to woo
    And to win you, though I love you so.

You are pale — or is it the moonlight's gleam
    That gives to your face that sorrowful look?
We must wake at last from our summer dream,
    We have come to the end of our tender book.
Love, the poet, has written well ;
    He has won our hearts by his poem sweet ;
And now, at the end, we must say farewell —
    Ah ! but the summer was fair and fleet.

Do you remember the night we met?
    You wore a rose in your amber hair ;
Closing my eyes I can see you yet,
    Just as you stood on the topmost stair,
A flutter of white from head to foot,
    A cluster of buds on your breast.   Ah, me !
But the vision was never half so sweet
    As it is to-night on my memory.

Hear the viol's cry, and the deep bassoon
    Seems sobbing out in its undertone,
Some sorrowful memory.   The tune
    Is the saddest one I have ever known.

Or is it because we must part to-night,
That the music seems so sad? Ah, me! —
You are weeping, love, and your lips are white —
The ways of life are a mystery.

I love you, love, with a love so true
That in coming years I shall not forget
The beautiful face and the dream I knew,
And memory always will hold regret.
I stand by the seas as I stand to-night,
And think of the summer whose blossoms died
When the frosts of fate fell chill and white
On the fairest flower of the summertide.

They are calling you — must I let you go?
Must I say good-by and go my way?
If we must part, it is better so —
Good-by's such a sorrowful word to say!
Give me, my darling, one last sweet kiss, —
So we kiss our dear ones and see them die;
But death holds no parting so sad as this; —
God bless you, and keep you, and so — good-by!

A THORN

AH love! thy love is like the flowers,
It fills my life with happy hours,
With color and perfume;
But if I pull the leaves aside
I find a grief I fain would hide,
A thorn among the blooms.

A FAREWELL

TOO rare a flower is love, its bloom to keep
  In the raw cold of our unlovely clime,
Too frail to thrive in this our weary time.
I would not have thy kisses, sweet, grow cheap
  Nor thy dear looks round out an idle rhyme, —
And so I say, let us loose hands and part;
Dear, with my hand you do not loose my heart.

Were it not sadder, in the years to come,
  To feel the hand-clasp slacken for long use,
  The untuned heart-strings for long stress refuse
To yield old harmonies, the songs grow dumb
  For weariness, and all the old spells lose
The first enchantment ?   Yet this thing must be.
Love is but mortal, save in Memory.

Sweet is the fragrance of remembered love ;
  The memory of clasped hands is very sweet,
  Joined hands that did not once too often meet
And never knew that saddest word " Enough ! "
  And so 'tis well that, ere our springtime fleet,
Thus in the hey-day of our love part we, —
Farewell, and all white omens go with thee !

CHANGES

WHOM first we love, you know, we seldom wed
  Time rules us all.   And life, indeed, is not
The thing we planned it out ere hope was dead —
  And then, we women cannot choose our lot.

132

Much must be borne which it is hard to bear:
   Much given away which it were sweet to keep —
God help us all! who need, indeed, His care.
   And yet, I know, the Shepherd loves His sheep.

My little boy begins to babble now
   Upon my knee his earliest infant prayer.
He has his father's eager eyes, I know,
   And, they say too, his mother's sunny hair.

But when he sleeps and smiles upon my knee,
   And I can feel his light breath come and go,
I think of one (Heaven help and pity me!)
   Who loved me, and whom I loved, long ago.

Who might have been . . . ah, what I dare not think!
   We all are changed. God judges for us best.
God help us do our duty and not shrink,
   And trust in heaven humbly for the rest.

But blame us women not, if some appear
   Too cold at times; and some too gay and light.
Some griefs gnaw deep; some woes are hard to bear;
   Who knows the Past? and who can judge us right?

Ah, were we judged by what we might have been,
   And not by what we are, too apt to fall! —
My little child — he sleeps and smiles between
   These thoughts and me. In Heaven we shall know
     all.

                 OWEN MEREDITH

WISTFUL

DEAR, it is hard to stand
       So near thy life, yet so apart.
So near — I think so near — thine heart;
So near that I could touch thine hand,
And yet so far I dare not take
That hand in mine for love's dear sake.

So near that I can look my fill
At stated times upon thy face,
So far that I must yield the place
To others, sore against my will,
So near that I can see thee smile,
So far, my poor heart aches the while.

Dear, it is hard to know,
Whate'er the stress, the storm, the strife,
The fret, the sadness of thy life,
I have no power, no right to show
Love in my heart, love on my lips,
To comfort thee in life's eclipse;

No right to claim before the rest,
The privilege to weep with thee;
No right across life's stormy sea,
To bid thee welcome to my breast;
No right to share thy hopes, thy fears,
Through all the weary, weary years.

Dear, it is hard to feel
That bliss may meet thee, full and fair,
Wherein poor I can have no share;

That the wide future may reveal
The joys of harvest manifold,
While I stand lonely in the cold.

Dear, it is hard.   But God doth know
How leal the heart that beats for thee ;
It is enough, enough for me
To love thee.   Let the future show
Love can live on for its own sake,
Though eyes may weep, though heart may ache.

A BROKEN SONNET

YOU loved me once, I know !
    I had the first, the best ; let others reap
The after-fruits, although it cost me pain ;
Although I sometimes turn aside and weep
To see Love's golden grainage scattered so ; —
Borne where each errant wind may chance to blow,—
The gift you gave you cannot take again.

You love me still, I know!
It is not possible you should forget
All I have been in the dear days gone by ;
For Time is strong, but Memory stronger yet
On his gray fortress walls doth greenly grow ;
You could not hate me if you would, and — O!
I loved, and I shall love you till I die !

CLO GRAVES

"FORGET thee?" If to dream by night,
  And muse on thee by day;
If all the worship deep and wild
  A lover's heart can pay;
If prayers in absence breathed for thee,
  To Heaven's protecting power,
If wingéd thoughts that flit to thee
  A thousand in an hour;
If busy Fancy blending thee
  With all my future lot, —
If this thou call'st "forgetting,"
  Thou indeed shalt be forgot.

"Forget thee?" Bid the forest birds
  Forget their sweetest tune;
"Forget thee?" Bid the sea forget
  To swell beneath the moon;
Bid thirsty flowers forget to drink
  The eve's refreshing dew;
Thyself forget thine own dear land
  And its mountains wild and blue;
Forget each old familiar face,
  Each long-remembered spot,
When these things are forgot by thee,
  Then thou shalt be forgot.

Keep, if thou wilt, thy maiden peace,
  Still calm and fancy-free,
For God forbid thy gladsome heart
  Should grow less glad for me;

Yet while thy heart is still unworn,
  Oh! bid not mine to rove,
But let it nurse its humble faith,
  And uncomplaining love ; —
If these preserved for patient years,
  At last avail me not,
Forget me then ; — but ne'er believe
  That thou canst be forgot !
JOHN MOULTRIE

TO ———

WHAT boots it that thine eye is bright,
  Thy bosom fair, thy footsteps light,
    Since I must never see
That eye beam brightly me to greet,
That step bound lightly me to meet,
    That bosom heave for me?

Albeit indifferent as thou art,
I would have clasped that icy heart
    As closely to my own
As he of old embraced the form,
Which grew beneath the kisses warm,
    When love gave life to stone.

How few in this cold world have met
The one of whom they dreamt ; — and yet
    To waste the dreary hours
In a lone wild were not such woe
As to have met that one, and know
    She never can be ours.
LORD DALLING

THE MAID I LOVED

THE maid I loved, and still shall love,
  What song of mine her praise may render?
All song could say, she stands above,
  Beyond all words, being dear and tender.
Bright as the stars, yet not so high;
  Fair as the moon, but far less fickle;
Sweet as the lovely months that lie
  Between the seedtime and the sickle.
Oh, were my vows like breezes shy,
  With fragrant sighs to breathe upon her—
Oh, were my hopes like flowers to lie
  About her path to do her honor—
Oh, were my voice a silver lyre
  To sound her praise and sing her glory—
My happiness and heart's desire
  Had not been now an ended story.

REMINISCENCE

IT was a summer eve, and underneath
  The shadowy trees you kissed me. In my heart
That moment came a new, fair world to light—
A world illumined by a rosy glow
Of new, fond thoughts, and passionate, sweet joy!

   *   *   *   *   *   *

When you were gone I doted o'er the thought
That you were mine, dear love! I pressed my hands
Above my throbbing heart, that beat so fast

THE MAID I LOVED

With knowledge of its own intense delight.
I slept and in my dreams you kissed me still.

* * * * * *

The sun rose fair.   I could not rest, but longed
To be alone among the fields and trees,
For I was stifled with sweet thoughts, and love
Ran riot in my heart. . . .   And as I walked,
The flowers, the birds, the breeze that floated by
All seemed to know my secret and to say :
" He loves you, loves you, loves you — only you ! "

* * * * * *

Ah, years have passed since then — and yet to-day
I still can thank the dear God over all
In that to me it once was given to know
Such perfect joy as in that hour when first
You kissed me, darling, and my heart awoke.

THY WITCHING LOOK

THY witching look is like a two-edged sword
    To pierce his heart by whom thou art surveyed :
Thy rosy lips the precious balm afford
    To heal the wound thy keen-edged sword has made.

I am its victim ; I have felt the steel ;
    My heart now rankles with the smarting pain ;
Give me thy lips the bitter wound to heal —
    Thy lips to kiss, and I am whole again.

From the Arabic

LOVE UNRETURNED

MY soul, where is the fruit of thy long pain
    To render to the husbandman above?
Thou hast been watered by my tears of love
For that pure spirit whose serene disdain
Pierced like a ploughshare through thee, leaving plain
    Forgotten depths wind-sown, whereout I strove
    Unceasingly to gather what might prove,
In time of harvest, tares instead of grain.

"Alas!" my soul said, "had but Love passed by
    And cast into the furrows as he went
    Sowing beside all waters, in the spring,
Methinks I had borne fruit abundantly
    For God to garner, as He sits intent
    Above the angels at their winnowing."

                    H. C. BEECHING

WANT

YOU swore you loved me all last June:
    And now December's come and gone.
The Summer went with you — too soon.
    The Winter goes — alone.

Next Spring the leaves will all be green;
    But love like ours once turned to pain,
Can be no more what it hath been,
    Though roses bloom again.

Return, return the unvalued wealth
   I gave! which scarcely profits you —
The heart's lost youth — the soul's lost health —
   In vain! . . . false friend, adieu!

I keep one faded violet
   Of all once ours, — you left no more.
What I have lost I may forget,
    But you cannot restore.

OWEN MEREDITH

WHEN TIME HATH BEREFT THEE

WHEN time hath bereft thee of charms now divine,
   When youth shall have left thee, nor beauty be
     thine,
When roses shall vanish that circle thee now
And the thorn thou wouldst banish shall press on thy
   brow,
   In the hour of thy sadness, then think upon me,
   And the thought shall be madness, deceiver, to thee.

When he who could turn thee from virtue and fame
Shall leave thee and spurn thee, to sorrow and shame,
When by him requited thy brain shall be stung,
Thy hope shall be blighted, thy bosom be wrung;
   In the depth of thy sadness, then think upon me,
   And the thought shall be madness, deceiver, to thee.

Old Song

GIVE ME MORE LOVE

GIVE me more love or more disdain;
   The torrid or the frozen zone
Brings equal ease unto my pain,
   The temperate affords me none;
Either extreme of love or hate
   Is better than a calm estate.

Give me a storm; if it be love,
   Like Danæ in a golden shower
I'll bathe in bliss; or if it prove
   Disdain, that torrent will devour
My vulture hopes; and he's possessed
   Of heaven that's but from hell released:
Then crown my joys or cure my pain;
   Give me more love or more disdain.

THOMAS CAREW

LOST AND FOUND

I LOST the brook as it wound its way
   Like a thread of silver hue;
Through greenwood and valley, through meadow gay,
   It was hidden from my view:
But I found it again in a noble river,
   Sparkling and broad and free,
Wider and fairer growing ever
   Till it reached the boundless sea.

I lost a tiny seed I sowed
   With many a sigh and tear,
And vainly waited through sunshine and cold
   For the young green to appear;
But surely after many long days
   The blossom and fruit will come,
And the reapers on high the sheaves will raise
   For a joyful harvest home.

I lost a love that made my life,
   A love that was all for me;
Oh, vainly I sought it amid the strife
   On this dark and raging sea:
But deeper and purer I know it waits
   Beyond my wistful eyes;
I shall find it again within the gates
   Of the garden of paradise.

LONGINGS

IF I could hold your hands to-night,
   Just for a little while, and know
That only I of all the world
   Possessed them so.

If I could see you here to-night,
   Between me and the twilight pale —
A slender shape in that old chair,
   So light and frail.

Your cool white dress, its foldings lost
   In one broad sweep of shadow gray;
Your weary head just dropped aside,
   That old sweet way.

Bowed like a flower-cup dashed with rain,
   The darkness crossing half your face,
And just the glimmer of a smile
   For one to trace.

If I could see your eyes, that reach
   Far out into the farthest sky,
Where past the trail of dying suns
   The old years lie.

If I could touch your lips to-night,
   And steal the sadness from their smile,
And find the last kiss they have kept
   This weary while!

If it could be — Oh, all in vain
    The restless trouble of my soul
Sets as the great tides of the main
    Toward your control !

In vain the longings of the lips,
    The eyes' desire and the pain ;
The hunger of the heart — O love,
    Is it in vain?

TOO LATE WE MET

TOO late we met, love, you and I,
    We may not now be loving ;
For should the heart indulge a sigh
    The conscience wakes reproving.
Ah, yes, too late! the die is cast,
    Our hearts must hide their sorrow ;
Farewell, this meeting is the last,
    We part for aye to-morrow.

Had we but met in earlier days,
    Ere other chains had bound us ;
Had Destiny but crossed our ways
    And Love unfettered found us ;
Life had not known its lonely past
    Nor feared a dreary setting,
Nor all our days been overcast
    With longing and regretting.
                              G. H. WESTLEY

145

ABSENCE

IN this fair stranger's eyes of gray
    Thine eyes, my love! I see.
I shiver; for the passing day
    Hath borne me far from thee.

This is the curse of life! that not
    A nobler, calmer train
Of wiser thoughts and feelings blot
    Our passions from our brain.

But each day brings its petty dust
    Our soon-choked souls to fill;
And we forget because we must,
    And not because we will.

MATTHEW ARNOLD

HER ROSES

AGAINST her mouth she pressed the rose. and there
    'Neath the caress of lips as soft and red
As its own petals, quick the bright bud spread
    And ope'd, and flung its fragrance on the air.
It ne'er again a bud's young grace can wear!
    O love, regret it not!   It gladly shed
Its soul for thee. and though thou kiss it dead
    It does not murmur at a fate so fair.

Thus, once, thou breath'dst on me, till every germ
    Of love and song broke into rapturous flower,
And sent a challenge upward to the sky.

What if too sweet fruition set a term
Too brief to all things? I have lived my hour,
And die contented, since for thee I die.

OWEN INNSLY

TO ———

IN years to come I ask thee not to say:
   "I loved him once; once I did hold him dear:"
Ah no ! long since I put that hope away,
And buried it in smiles, without a tear.
But say: "'Mid all who worshipped at my feet
Exalting me, 'mid all who loved me best,
As I remember now, I think there beat
No heart more fondly in a single breast,
No eye that brightened quicker when I came,
No hand that lay more longingly in mine,
No voice that knew a tenderer tone to name
My name than his whose love seemed half divine."
If this thou say, though I be dead the while,
The words will reach me; I shall hear, and smile.

OWEN INNSLY

Love makes our darkest days
In golden suns go down!
So let us clothe our hearts with love
And crown us with Love's crown.

GERALD MASSEY

THOU CANST NOT FORGET

THOU canst not forget me, for memory will fling
    Her light o'er oblivion's dark sea;
And where'er thou roamest a something will cling
    To thy bosom that whispers of me.
Though the chords of thy spirit I never may sweep,
    Of my touch they'll retain a soft thrill,
Like the low undertone of the murmuring deep
    When the wind that has stirred it is still.

The love that is kept in the beauty of trust,
    Cannot pass like the foam from the seas,
Or a mark that the finger hath made in the dust,
    When 'tis swept by the breath of the breeze.
They tell me my love thou wilt calmly resign,
    Yet I ever, while listening to them,
Will sigh for the heart that was linked unto mine
    As a rosebud is linked to its stem.

Thou canst not forget me! Too long hast thou flung
    Thy spirit's soft pinions o'er mine;
Too deep was the promise that round my lips clung,
    As they softly responded to thine.
In the dusk of the twilight, beneath the blue sky,
    My presence will mantle thy soul,
And a feeling of sadness will rush to thine eye,
    Too deep for thy manhood's control.

Thou canst not forget me! The passion that dwelt
    In thy bosom will slumbering lie,
In the memory of all thou hast murmured and felt

The thought of me never can die.
Thou mayst turn to another, and wish to forget,
But the wish will not bring thee repose;
For, oh! thou wilt find that the thorns of regret
Were but hid by the leaves of the rose.

BY A VIRGINIA LADY

OLD SONG

THE minstrel touched his silver strings
His voice rose clear and free,
And like a wilding bird that sings
Poured forth his melody;
He sang of Love, that wondrous power
To torture and to fret —
Oh what is Love — what does Love mean?
Regret, sweetheart, regret.

So pluck the wild rose from the tree —
Ere long 'twill fade away;
So cage some bright-winged butterfly
To die with parting day;
They are more lasting yet than Love
That heart-bewitching snare —
For what is Love — what does Love mean?
Despair, sweetheart, despair.

Pains of love be sweeter far
Than all other pleasures are.

DRYDEN

THE PAIN OF LOVE

A MIGHTY pain to love it is,
  And 'tis a pain that pain to miss.
But of all pains, the greatest pain
It is to love, and love in vain.

*   *   *   *   *   *

Love in her sunny eyes does basking play;
Love walks the pleasant mazes of her hair;
Love does on both her lips forever stray,
And sows and reaps a thousand kisses there;
In all her outward parts Love's always seen,
But oh! he never went within.

ABRAHAM COWLEY

VALE!

GOOD–BY, good-by! I have no chain to hold you,
  No soft spun web of love wherein to fold you;
You wove the web that you have riven apart,
  And so — good-by, sweetheart!

It was your eyes, dear, not my lips deceived you;
You told their tale, and I, alas, believed you,
Who said I had gold hair and eyes of blue,
  And was the world to you.

Now that your eyes forget their foolish story,
Straight falls from me my borrowed crown of glory;
My eyes are gray and colorless my hair —
  Just as they always were.

And I — (who was the world to you — you swore it!)
Have known a world's delight, and thank God for it.
What's left of life is little enough to pay
      For one imperial day.

"Tis given to man to mix with men and let
   Strong worldly clamors drown his spirits cry:
   The woman only can regret, regret,
   And wearied with regretting, yearn to die."

   "Though Fate may part and seas may sever,
   Love for an hour is love forever."

IV

LOVE'S NIGHT

To know, to esteem, to love — and then to part,
Makes up life's tale to many a feeling heart.

S. T. COLERIDGE

Alas, how easily things go wrong !
A sigh too much or a kiss too long ;
There comes a mist and a blinding rain,
And things are never the same again.

ALAS THE SONGS!

ALAS the songs ! — the songs of Love and Youth —
   The burgeoning of Spring !
Give ye no ear ! no ear ! For Love in truth,
   Love is a bitter thing.

Sorrow of unborn years to him who sips
   Of that sweet stinging wine.
What savor now thereof upon *our* lips —
   On mine and thine?

Once did we quaff the juice intoxicate
   With promise of the years.
" Bide ye the lees !" they cried. We let them prate.
   We had no fears.

The end has fallen upon us over-soon,
   The promise is forsworn.
The day should yet be high : 'tis afternoon ;
   And Night is born.

JOHN W. DE LYS

DEAR, it is twilight time, the time of rest;
   Ah! cease that weary pacing to and fro;
Sit down beside me in this cushioned nest,
   Warm with the brightness of our ingle-glow.
Dear, thou art troubled.   Let me share thy lot
   Of shadow, as I shared thy sunshine hours.
I am no child, though childhood, half forgot,
   Lies close behind me, with its toys and flowers.
I am a woman waked by happy love
   To keep home's sacred altar-fire alight!
Thou hast elected me to stand above
   All others in thine heart.   I claim my right.
Not wife alone, but mate and comrade true;
I shared thy roses, let me share thy rue!

Bitter?   I know it.   God hath made it so.
   But from his hand shall we take good alone
And evil never?   Let the world's wealth go.
   Life hath no loss which love cannot atone.
Show me the new hard path that we must tread.
   I shall not faint, nor falter by the way;
And be there cloud or sunshine overhead.
   I shall not fail thee to my dying day.
But love me, love me, let our hearts and lips
   Cling closer in our sorrow than in joy;
Let faith outshine our fortunes in eclipse,
   And love deem wealth a lost and broken toy.
Joy made us glad, let sorrow find us true
God blessed our roses, He will bless our rue!

LIFE'S UNEXPRESSED

THERE are sweeter words than were ever said,
  And sweeter songs than were ever sung,
And fonder tears than were ever shed
  By the eyes of the old or the hearts of the young

For the love that speaks is the love that dies,
  And soonest yields unto Time's control;
But the deathless love is the love that lies
  Deeply enshrined in the speechless soul.

For the tenderest music the spirit knows
  Is the music that cannot be expressed.
And the fondest tears of man are those
  That lie unwept in his breaking breast.

For the soul is strong and the flesh is weak,
  And fonder far than the words we hear
Are the words our lips refuse to speak
  When they whom our souls love best are near.

Ah me! to think that it must be so!
  To think, ah me! in the morning light
That the hearts we love must never know
  The tears we weep through the lonely night!

Ah! ever thus with the old and young,
  Till both are laid with the quiet dead,
The sweetest songs must remain unsung,
  And the fondest words remain unsaid.
                              ANNE ELDERS

SEPARATION

IF it were land, oh, weary feet could travel,
　　If it were sea, a ship might cleave the wave,
If it were Death, sad Love could look to heaven,
And see through tears the sunlight on the grave.
　　Not land, or sea, or death keeps us apart
　　But only thou, oh unforgiving Heart.

If it were land, through piercing thorns I'd travel,
If it were sea, I'd cross to thee, or die,
If it were Death, I'd tear Life's veil asunder
That I might see thee with a clearer eye.
　　Ah none of these could keep our souls apart —
　　Forget, forgive, oh unforgiving Heart.

ANNE REEVE ALDRICH

DE PROFUNDIS

DEAR and desired above all things that are;
　　More dear than life, and more desired than death,
Fairer than June — more sweet than April's breath,
More unattainable than any star !

I move below you in the world of men,
　　And work and wait and love you all the time,
　　Bidding my heart mock, in a peal of rhyme,
Its own wild prayer to be beloved again.

Since in your world of light, and strength and peace
　　You move, untouched by our poor hopes and fears.
　　Why do I send this song to vex your ears?
Why cross your sunlight with such words as these?

Because — worth goes not always vowed to worth,
   And Life and Death both come to those who wait;
   April and June come, though they tarry late;
And sometimes stars grow kind, and stoop to earth.

LOVE NOT

LOVE not, love not! ye hapless sons of clay!
   Hope's gayest wreaths are made of earthly
      flowers, —
Things that are made to fade and fall away
Ere they have blossomed for a few short hours.
                              Love not!

Love not! The thing you love may change,
The rosy lip may cease to smile on you,
The kindly beaming eye grow cold and strange,
The heart still warmly beat, yet not be true.
                              Love not!

Love not! The thing you love may die, —
May perish from the gay and gladsome earth;
The silent stars, the blue and smiling sky,
Beam o'er its grave, as once upon its birth.
                              Love not!

Love not! Oh, warning vainly said
In present hours as in the years gone by!
Love flings a halo round the dear one's head
Faultless, immortal, till they change or die.
                              Love not!
                    HON. MRS. NORTON

NO! let me alone — 'tis better so,
   My way and yours are widely far apart.
Why should you stop to grieve about my woe?
And why should I not step across your heart?
A man's heart is a poor thing at the best,
And yours is no whit better than the rest.

I loved you once! Ah, yes! Perhaps I did.
Women are curious things, you know, and strange,
And hard to understand, and then besides,
The key of her soul's music oft doth change,
And so — ah! do not look at me that way!
I loved you once, but that was yesterday!

Sometimes a careless word doth rankle deep —
So deep that it can change a heart like this,
And blot out all the long sweet throbbing hours
That went before, crowned gold with rapturous bliss;
So deep that it can blot out hours divine,
And make a heart as hard and cold as mine.

Nay, do not speak, I never can forget:
So let us say good-by and go our ways;
Mayhap the pansies will start from the dust
Of our past days — the slumbrous happy days
When I was trusting, and life knew no grief,
But blossomed with my clinging, sweet belief.

Good-by! good-by! Part of my life you take,
Its fairest part. Nay, do not touch my lips.
Once they were yours, but now, oh, my lost love!

I would not have you touch my finger tips,
And saying this I feel no chill of pain,
I cannot even weep above my slain.

If God cares aught for women who have loved
And worshipped idols false, I trust He will
Keep us so far apart that never more
Our paths may cross.   Why are you standing still?
Good-by, I say.   This is the day's dim close ;
Our love is no more worth than last year's rose.

LAST WORDS

YOU can write down sweet words in a letter,
    And try to send love by the post ;
You can tell me how vastly 'tis better
    To have played the game Love, though we've lost.

You say you are wretched without me :
    Have you ever thought what I endure?
The sickening pain — ah ! don't doubt me —
    Which not even your presence could cure.

For you know that our passionate yearning
    Can never be satisfied here ;
In the long lane of Life, there's no turning
    That I see, which will bring us more near.

By one act of folly once parted
    We must live out our lives, you and I ;
And though we are both broken-hearted,
    Let us whisper, good-by, love, good-by.

163

A FALSE STEP

SWEET, thou hast trod on a heart.
   Pass! there's a world full of men.
And women as fair as thou art
   Must do such things now and then.

Thou hast only stepped unaware, —
   Malice, not one can impute;
And why should a heart have been there
   In the way of a fair woman's foot?

It was not a stone that could trip,
   Nor was it a thorn that could rend:
Put up thy proud underlip!
   'Twas merely the heart of a friend.

MRS. E. B. BROWNING

A LOVE-LETTER

MY love — my chosen — but not mine! I send
   My whole heart to thee in these words I write:
So let the blotted lines, my soul's sole friend
   Lie upon thine, and there be blest at night.

   *   *   *   *   *   *

My darling, I have loved you as men love
   Light, music, odor, beauty, love itself; —
Whatever is apart from and above
   Those daily needs which deal with dust and pelf.

My wildest wish was vassal to thy will.
  My haughtiest hope a pensioner on thy smile,
Which did with light my barren being fill,
  As moonlight glorifies some desert isle.

I never thought to know what I have known —
  The rapture, dear, of being loved by you:
I never thought within my heart to own
  One wish so blest that you should share it too.

    *   *   *   *   *   *

Perchance I shall not ever see again
  Your face.   I know that I shall never see
Its radiant beauty as I saw it then,
  Save by this lonely lamp of memory.

Farewell, and yet again farewell, and yet
  Never farewell — if farewell mean to fare
Alone and disunited.   Love hath set
  Our days in music to the self-same air.

    *   *   *   *   *   *

Man cannot make, but may ennoble fate
  By nobly bearing it.   So let us trust
Not to ourselves but God, and calmly wait
  Love's orient, out of darkness and of dust.

OWEN MEREDITH

TWILIGHT and trees,
　A soft cool air that blows from the west,
The clear wide vault of an open sky,
The tender twitter of birds in their nest —
　And a memory.

　Is it so long
Since I kissed your lips and your snow-cold brow?
　I had sinned with a laugh in my soul before;
But I loved you then, as I love you now
　And forever more.

　Is it lonely in heaven?
Dear heart, in the blaze of that shining throng
　Of deathless souls. do you sometimes wait
For another's voice to join in the song
　That he learned too late?

　Have pity. God!
If I cannot be where my darling is,
　If my scarlet sinning is past regret,
For the sake of sorrow, grant only this.
　That she may forget.

GOOD-BY

GOOD-BY, dear eyes; a little while
　You lit the darkness of my days;
　Now life is naught, and nothing stays;
Good-by, dear eyes, and tender smile
　And loving ways.

Good-by, dear hands ; and now I press
    For the last time your whiteness slim
    And if my eyes with tears are dim,
You will not love them, dear, the less
    For tears in them.

Good-by, dear lips, where Death has set
    His kiss, a colder one than thine ;
    But in your dwelling-place divine,
Shall you. dear love, one hour forget
    This kiss of mine?

A WOMAN'S ANSWER

LAST year I was yours for a look or a word —
    Yours, body and soul ; yours for evil or good.
But to-day I could meet you with pulses unstirred,
    Unimpassioned in mood.

Had you chosen to speak in those days that are gone,
    Yours was it to speak, it could never be mine —
Now the hour is over, the dream now is done.
    Can it be you repine?

Is it strange, do you think, that my love has grown cold,
    Starved to death, for the lack of a word, of a smile?
Once it might have been yours, friend, to have and to
      hold,
    Had you thought it worth while.
LYDIA M. WOOD

HAST THOU FORGOTTEN ME

HAST thou forgotten me?   The days are dark,
Light ebbs from heaven, and songless soars the
   lark;
Vexed like my heart, loud moans the unquiet sea —
         Hast thou forgotten me?

Hast thou forgotten me?   O dead delight
Whose dreams and memories torture me at night —
O love — my life !   O sweet, so fair to see !
         Hast thou forgotten me?

Hast thou forgotten?   Lo, if one should say —
Noontide were night, or night were flaming day —
Grief blinds mine eyes, I know not which it be!
         Hast thou forgotten me?

Hast thou forgotten?   Ah ! if Death should come,
Close my sad eyes, and charm my song-bird dumb, —
Tired of strange woes — my fate were hailed with glee —
         Hast thou forgotten me?

Hast thou forgotten me?   What joy have I?
A dim blown bird beneath an alien sky, —
O that on mighty pinions I could flee —
         Hast thou forgotten me?

Hast thou forgotten?   Yea, Love's horoscope
Is blurred with tears and suffering beyond hope —
Ah ! like dead leaves forsaken of the tree.
         Thou hast forgotten me !

Philip J. Holdsworth

ONLY FOR THIS

WAS it for this, dear heart, we met —
　　You and I, in that May-time sweet —
Met and lingered with careless feet,
Till love-lit eyes with tears grew wet,
　　Only to dream of a vanished bliss —
　　　　Only for this?

Was it for this the days were bright,
　　Flow'rs so gay and skies so blue?
　　Was it for this the love we knew
Touched all the world with golden light,
　　Only to grieve for the love we miss —
　　　　Only for this?

Was it for this we parted, dear,
　　You and I, in such sore distress,
　　Whisp'ring our vows with fond caress,
Dreaming of love 'mid every tear,
　　Only to sigh for that farewell kiss —
　　　　Only for this?

Only to watch with bitter woe
　　Year after year the May flowers bloom?
　　Only to miss through sun and gloom
One face — one voice of long ago?
　　Only to dream of a vanished bliss —
　　　　Only for this?

Louisa Jackson

REGRETS

IF we had but known, if we had but known,
 Those summer days together,
That one would stand next year alone,
In the blazing July weather!
Why, we trifled away the golden hours
With gladness and beauty and calm,
Watching the glory of blossoming flowers,
Breathing the warm air's balm,
Seeing the children like sunbeams play
In the glades of the long cool wood;
Hearing the wild birds carol gay,
And the song of the murmuring flood.
Rich gems to Time's pitiless river thrown —
If we had but known. if we had but known!

If we had but known, if we had but known,
Those winter nights together,
How one would sit by the hearth alone
In the next December weather!
Why, we sped those last hours each for each,
With music, and games, and talk,
The careless, bright, delicious speech,
With no doubt or fear to balk.
Touching on all things grave and gay
With the freedom of two in one,
Yet leaving, as happy people may,
So much unsaid, undone.
Ah, priceless hours forever flown.
If we had but known, if we had but known!

If we had but known, if we had but known,
While yet we stood together,
How a thoughtless look, a slighting touch
Would sting and jar forever !
Cold lies the turf for the burning kiss,
The cross stands deaf to cries,
Dull as the wall of silence is
Are the gray unanswering skies !
We can never unsay the thing we said,
While the weary life drags past ;
We can never stanch the wound that bled
Where a chance stroke struck it last.
Oh, the patient love 'neath the heavy stone —
If we had but known, if we had but known !

.

AFTER LOVE

O TO part now, and parting now,
Never to meet again ;
To have done forever, I and thou,
With joy and so with pain.

It is too hard, too hard to meet
As friends and love no more ;
Those other meetings were too sweet
That went before.

And I would have, now love is over,
An end to all, an end :
I cannot, having been your lover,
Stoop to become your friend.

ARTHUR SYMONS

171

LIFE'S PITY

I THINK the pity of this life is love;
For from our love we gather all life's pain,
   And place too oft our hearts on earthly shrines
Where we would kneel — but where, alas, we fall
Beneath a shadow ever past recall;
   We seek for gold, when 'tis but dross that shines.
Then — if we may not turn our hearts above —
I *know* the pity of this life is love.

FOREVER

TWO human lives, two kindred hearts,
   By Destiny's decree
Met in the spring of life, to learn
   Its deepest mystery.
They dreamed their morning dreams of hope
   Through fair unclouded weather;
They opened love's bewitching book
   And read it through together;
They saw in one another's eyes
   A deep unspoken bliss;
And from each other's lips they took
   Love's ever-ready kiss.

And then the fate that crushes all
   The sweetest pleasures here,
Turned hope's glad music to a sigh,
   Its glory to a tear.
It stepped between them; ah! it mocked
   The love it could not kill;

It bade them in its fury live,
  And love, and suffer still.
They tried with outstretched hands to span
  Fate's wide, unyielding "Never."
The voice of Destiny replied:
  "Forever and forever."

ELIZABETH BERRY

ROSES

A CRIMSON rosebud into beauty breaking,
  A hand outstretched to pluck it ere it fall,
An hour of triumph and a sad forsaking
And then a withered roseleaf — that is all.

A maiden heart that knoweth not love's darting,
  A voice that teacheth love beyond recall,
An hour of joy, an hour of bitter parting,
  And then a broken heart — and that is all.

THREE, only three, my darling,
  Separate, solemn, slow;
Not like the swift and joyous ones
  We used to know,
When we kissed because we loved each other
  Simply to taste love's sweet,
And lavished our kisses as the summer
  Lavishes heat;
But as they kiss whose hearts are wrung,
  When hope and fear are spent,
And nothing is left to give, except
  A sacrament!

First of the three, my darling,
  Is sacred unto pain;
We have hurt each other often,
  We shall again,
When we pine because we miss each other,
  And do not understand
How the written words are much colder
  Than eye and hand.
I kiss thee, dear, for all such pain
  Which we may give or take;
Buried, forgiven before it comes,
  For our love's sake.

The second kiss, my darling;
  Is full of joy's sweet thrill:
We have blessed each other always,
  We always will.

We shall reach until we feel each other
  Beyond all time and space;
We shall listen till we hear each other
  In every place;
The earth is full of messengers,
  Which love sends to and fro; —
I kiss thee, darling, for all joy
  Which we shall know!

The last kiss, oh! my darling —
  My love — I cannot see,
Through my tears, as I remember
  What it may be.
We may die and never see each other,
  Die with no time to give
Any sign that our hearts are faithful
  To die, as live.
Token of what they will not see
  Who see our parting breath,
This one last kiss, my darling,
  The seal of death!

AGNES E. GLASE

INCOMPLETENESS

I HAVE another life I long to meet,
  Without which life, my life is incomplete.
O sweeter self! like me art thou astray?
Trying with all thy heart to find the way
To mine?   Straying like mine to find the breast
On which alone can weary heart find rest.

OCTAVE FEUILLET

DESERTED

AH, was it nobly done of him, if he
   Could love me not, to speak of love so well?
With fervent eloquence checked back with scorn
   The highest and the truest love to tell?
         Who had no love to give.

Why did he bend his eyes on me at times,
   Reluctantly, yet lovingly withal?
Take both my hands in his and calmly speak
   Wise words of counsel, that were so much gall?
         Who had no love to give.

And smile sometimes, a bland indulgent smile,
   While listening to the passion of my speech;
Lifting his brows, too, with a strange surprise,
   Standing so far above me, out of reach,
         Who had no love to give.

*   *   *   *   *   *

Ah, well! He cannot say to-day that I
   Most fully do not understand, whose life
Has been torn up by root and branch, to strew
   The fairest flowers in his path so rife,
         Who had no love to give.

Youth could not hold me back. All wisdom died
   My heart's love budded in the bleakest air;
And, frozen with the coldness of his smile,
   He turned away and let it perish there,
         Who had no love to give.

*   *   *   *   *   *

DESERTED

Does the heart's core send forth such blossoms twice?
  The gods are not so cruel, life so hard —
Ah, no ! for such love has no second fruits :
  Lives do not bloom again, so deeply scarred —
        I have no love to give.
                ETHEL DE FONBLANQUE

A CYCLE

IF he had come in the early dawn,
  When the sunrise flushed the earth,
I would have given him all my heart,
  Whatever the heart was worth.

If he had come in the noontide hour,
  He would not have come too late ;
I would have given him patient faith,
  For then I had learned to wait.

If he had come in the after-glow,
  In the peace of eventide,
I would have given him hands and brain
  And worked for him till I died.

If he comes now that the sun has set
  And the light has died away,
I will not give him a broken life
  But will turn and say him, " Nay ! "
                C. BROOKE

THERE are some hearts that, like the roving vine,
   Cling to unkindly rocks and ruined towers,
Spirits that suffer and do not repine —
   Patient and sweet as lowly-trodden flowers
That from the passer's heel arise
And fling back odorous breath instead of sighs.

Why should the heavy foot of sorrow press
   The willing heart of uncomplaining love —
Meek charity that shrinks not from distress,
   Gentleness, loth her tyrants to reprove?
Though virtue weep forever and lament,
Will one hard heart turn to her and repent?

Why should the reed be broken that will bend,
   And they that dry the tears in others' eyes
Feel their own anguish swelling without end.
   Their summer darkened with a smoke of sighs?
Sure, love to some fair region of his own
Will flee at last, and leave us here alone.

Love weepeth always — weepeth for the past,
   For woes that are, for woes that may betide;
Why should not hard ambition weep at last,
   Envy and hatred, avarice and pride?
Fate whispers, Sorrow is your lot:
They would be rebels: love rebelleth not.

   Love's of itself too sweet; the best of all
   Is when love's honey has a dash of gall.
                     HERRICK

FORBIDDEN

O WEARY feet that on Life's stony ways
    Must tread in separate paths; while Time's dark
        wings
Beat out the lagging hours of all the days,
    Marking the epochs of their wandering !
O lonely road !   O tired, pacing feet
            That may not meet.

O longing hands that may not, must not, clasp
    Those other loved ones in the world's wide night;
O parted hands that may not, must not, grasp
    Those other hands with yearnings infinite !
O starving lips, whose hunger is but this —
            They may not kiss.

O aching eyes that shine so far apart,
    Love-haunted eyes that may not, must not, tell
The secret of the passion-laden heart,
    The whispered secret that they know so well !
O hopeless love, that hope of death survives
            In such cleft lives !

O souls that never while the world rolls on
    Shall mingle in a speechless ecstasy !
O love that lives on hours long dead and gone —
    Bound love that strives so vainly to be free !
O joy of life that cometh all too late !
            O cruel fate !

PARTING WORDS

FAREWELL, farewell, my dream is o'er,
  I ask no parting token;
Nor would I clasp thy hand before
  My last farewell is spoken.
How coldly fair thy thrice-false face
  Dawns on my sad awaking,
No anguish there mine eyes can trace,
  Though this fond heart is breaking.

Be as thou wert before we met;
  Heave not one sigh, but leave me;
These studied looks, that feigned regret,
  Can nevermore deceive me.
The faltering tones that mock me so,
  Betray the fears that move thee;
Cease to degrade thy manhood. — Go!
  I scorn thee while I love thee.

Shall I forget the rapturous hours
  Of my too radiant morning —
The hand that culled the dewy flowers
  My girlish brow adorning?
Ah, no! for she who scorns thee now
  Will miss its dear caresses;
And sorrow to remember how
  It decks another's tresses.

Alas! this tortured soul of mine,
  Though by thy treason riven,
Can never cast thee from its shrine
  Unwept and unforgiven.

Nay, I, when youth and hope depart,
 The mournful willow wearing,
Must still deplore that shallow heart
 That was not worth the sharing.

The world thou hast deceived so long
 May smile on thee to-morrow;
While I alone must bear the wrong,
 The bitterness and sorrow!
O cruel world! O world unjust!
 That passes by unheeding,
Where love betrayed and blasted trust
 Low in the dust lie bleeding!

Go thou thy way! O heartless one!—
 Yet stay, a moment only!
How shall I face when thou art gone.
 The world, so vast, so lonely?
The words are like my passing knell:
 Ah me, and must we sever?
Forget that I have loved thee well—
 Adieu! adieu forever!

A LOVE'S LIFE

'TWAS Springtime of the day and year,
 Clouds of white fragrance hid the thorn.
My heart unto her heart drew near,
 And ere the dew had fled the morn,
  Sweet Love was born.

An August noon, an hour of bliss
 That stands amid my hours alone.
A word. a look, then — ah, that kiss !
 Joy's veil was rent, her secret known:
  Love was full grown.

And now this drear November eve,
 What has to-day seen done, heard said?
It boots not; who has tears to grieve
 For that last leaf yon tree has shed,
  Or for Love dead?

BURNT OUT

ONE word and only one,
 Before I go !
One sigh and all is done!
 Alas, not so!

Though Love that was my light
 Is lost for aye,
My course is set too right
 To swerve or stray.

Though Love be clean put out
    Yet must I run,
A lifeless world about
    A lightless sun.

THE AWAKENED

TAKE back all the words thou hast breathed in my
        ear.
Take back the fond glance of thy love-lighted eye, —
No longer, my heart, throb with hope nor with fear,
    No longer, my breast, heave affection's warm sigh.

Yet think not, thou false one, that dark and forlorn
    The path of the future to me shall still be,
Though the bright visions of life's early morn
    Have been dimm'd and been darkened by thee.

My soul shall arise exalted and pure
    Unstained by thy falsehood, unharmed by thy art,
And virtue triumphant with me shall endure
    And heal all the anguish of this wounded heart.
                              ELIZABETH HAZARD

    A pressing lover seldom lacks success,
    Whilst the respectful, like the Greek, sits down
    And wastes a ten years' siege before one town.
                              NICHOLAS ROWE

FINIS

THE end draws near.   By Fates unseen directed
    Our paths diverging tend.
To lives monotonous the Unexpected
    Comes as a friend,
While for a moment joyous smiles of meeting
    The gathering shades dispel.
Ave et Vale!   Lo! the ancient greeting,
    Hail, and Farewell!

A moment more!   And sadness follows after,
    In bursts of keen regret
That put to silence all the happy laughter
    Wherewith we met.
The past is dead, the present swiftly fading,
    And in the future dwell
Hopes faint and few, our longing glance evading.
    Hail, and Farewell!

The time has come!   'Mid alien scenes and faces
    Our lessening lives must lie,
And pass henceforth through solitary places
    Beneath a stormy sky.
Clasp hands, dear friend!   Against our best endeavor,
    The tides of Memory swell.
Part we as those who part indeed forever.
    Hail, and Farewell!

INDEX OF AUTHORS

185

186